A FORTUNE FOR
MY LADY

A FORTUNE FOR MY LADY

John Scurr

Book Guild Publishing
Sussex, England

First published in Great Britain in 2011 by
The Book Guild
Pavilion View
19 New Road
Brighton, BN1 1UF

Typesetting in Baskerville by
Keyboard Services, Luton, Bedfordshire

Printed in Great Britain by
CPI Antony Rowe

A catalogue record for this book is available from
The British Library

ISBN 978 1 84624 535 0

People in love are sad, and many times weep.

James Howard, *The English Monsieur,* **1666**

Preface

It took me a whole week to fall in love with Lady Corinne Malvor. With both Mary and Harriet I had been instantly smitten, but my love for Corinne crept up on me insidiously and then took possession of my soul all of a sudden, just when I had begun foolishly to assume that I had at last become the master of my fate. But before I say any more, let me first introduce myself to those readers who have the misfortune not to have read my previous memoir, *A Pirate for Harriet*.

My name is Nathaniel Devarre. I was born on 10 April 1642 in the London ward of Billingsgate to a gentle mother, who died giving birth to me. My severe and fiery father was a minister of the Presbyterian Church and I grew up with two elder sisters who treated me with disdain. After completing my education at the Greencoat School, my ambition was to earn my living as a portrait painter, but my father would have none of it and obtained for me an appointment as a purser in the Commonwealth Navy. I found my new life at sea most disagreeable, but after the Restoration of King Charles II, I was nonetheless promoted to Master. In June 1666, during an unexpected encounter with the Dutch fleet off the coast of Flanders, I withdrew my ship, the *Invincible*, from a very uneven battle, after Captain Abercorn was severely wounded. I was subsequently convicted by the Admiralty of cowardice and sentenced to death. After the intervention of Lord Abercorn, who believed my withdrawal from action had saved the lives of his son and many others, the death sentence was lifted, but I was dishonourably discharged from the Navy.

My father and two sisters had all perished in the great plague of 1665. Being thus the sole beneficiary of my father's will, I inherited the substantial wealth he had accumulated from his various investments. Consequently, I purchased a six-roomed stone house in the village of Highgate, which is situated on a four hundred-foot hill, five miles or so to the north of London. Fortunately, my home contained only two hearths, so my Hearth Tax was not excessive: only four shillings per annum. The village boasted more than one hundred and sixty houses and cottages, spread mainly around the village green and the top of the hill. The village also contained five inns, several alehouses, a chapel, a Presbyterian meeting house, almshouses and a bequest school for poor boys. It was indeed a most pleasant place to live, owing both to its fresh country air and freedom of worship for non-Anglicans, being outside the five-mile limit of the capital.

I now resolved to fulfil my earlier ambition to be a portrait painter. Regrettably, my few customers were not always satisfied with my depictions of them and sometimes refused to purchase the completed works, so that the financial returns of my labour were not great. But, fortunately, my inheritance ensured that I was able to live comfortably with only a small income from painting. The knowledge of my dubious artistic ability, my dishonourable discharge from the Navy and the eccentricity of my living alone, employing no servants and never wearing the fashionable periwig, all earned me the contempt of many of the village residents. And none was more disdainful than Mary Blakeney, the young lady with whom I was hopelessly in love.

Lady Corinne Malvor first came into my life in August 1667 when she commissioned me to paint a portrait of her reclining upon her bed. This resulted in my having to kill her husband, Sir Frederick, in a duel, after he had falsely accused me of having an affair with his wife. Nine months later, the Malvor family again came ominously to my attention when Lord Abercorn employed me to go to Jamaica to bring back his daughter, Harriet, who had eloped with Sir Frederick's younger brother, Darby.

In Port Royal, Jamaica, I was befriended by the formidable buccaneer, Captain Jonathon Kincaid, and a Scottish one-time whore, known only as Nancy, who was the proprietor of the Sea Horse Tavern. I soon found myself involved in intrigue, piracy and a succession of tragedies, a detailed knowledge of which is not essential for understanding the story I am now relating. I advise those new readers who might wish to know more to spend the four pence required to purchase a copy of my previous memoir.

The outcome of it all was that I fell in love with Lady Harriet Abercorn just prior to her sudden demise, and returned home in September 1668, bent on taking revenge on Darby Malvor. Holding Darby responsible for Harriet's death, I killed him one night in a fair fight upon the staircase of Lady Corinne Malvor's mansion. In addition to being Corinne's brother-in-law, Darby had also been her most recent lover, but at that time was very much out of her favour.

Four days later, to my great surprise, Mary Blakeney – resident of Highgate village and recipient of my unrequited love – fearfully advised me of her father's scheme to offer me her hand in marriage in exchange for the investment of a substantial amount of my remaining wealth in his ailing food importing business. Despite the painful remorse that continued to haunt me after the loss of my beloved Harriet, I was still very much in love with Mary, but, realising her deep aversion to me, my honour required that I reject this offered fulfilment of my cherished dream.

A month later, I presented Lady Corinne Malvor with a three-row pearl necklace I had brought back from my disastrous adventure on the Spanish Main, and she consequently granted me her warm and willing intimacy.

Readers of *A Pirate for Harriet* will recall that at this point my previous memoir concluded.

1

Corinne was, in fact, the first woman with whom I had ever shared a bed. I was then twenty-six years old, but the strong religious convictions, relentlessly instilled in me by my clerical father, had previously inhibited me from carnal experience. Not that I had received many invitations of that nature. Although I considered myself to be quite presentable – having shoulder-length, wavy dark brown hair, brown eyes, a fairly straight nose and a slim moustache – I seemed to be lacking in whatever was required to set ladies' hearts a-flutter. Indeed, Mary Blakeney had once said to me, 'I can assure you that there is absolutely nothing about your appearance or demeanour which I find remotely appealing.' Poor me!

Nevertheless, Corinne enjoyed my company and, indeed, was very fond of me. But she certainly wasn't in love with me and never pretended otherwise. There was, however, never any doubt about *my* feelings. My love for her swiftly developed into a deep and overwhelming passion which soon considerably reduced the lingering distress of my earlier amorous failures.

I frequently travelled to London by public stage coach, either to paint portraits of persons who had responded to my advertisements or, more often, to visit Corinne. It never ceased to surprise me that, after the plague and the fire, half a million people continued to live in that filthy, reeking city. The majority of the other five and a half million of England's population wisely lived in villages and small market towns as the predominantly agricultural

5

economy dictated. Under the reign of Charles II, the rapid growth of merchant shipping and overseas trade had contributed to substantial rises in wages and in payments made to the poor relief system. Yet there was still deprivation and poverty, very noticeable in parts of London. As many as five families might live in one squalid dwelling on a narrow, cobbled street strewn with garbage and polluted by the constant stench of smoke and open sewers. The Malvor mansion, of course, stood in the fashionable and pleasant St James's Square.

On the days that I remained at home in Highgate, writing my memoir of my quest for Harriet, I would spare an hour or two to sup ale in the local taverns or stroll in the meadows and woodlands around the village. My two friends, Jeremy Grenville and Timothy Cottle, regularly provided good company when drinking in the Gatehouse Tavern, but I was equally content when alone with my thoughts.

As for Mary, she and her father departed the village shortly before Christmas 1668. Timothy, who was always well versed in both information and gossip, informed me that Mr Blakeney had had to sell his brick mansion on the Toll Road, owing to his deteriorating financial situation, and that he now rented a small property in Duck Lane, London. His food importing business had apparently been dissolved. Since then, I had heard no more of Mary but often wondered how she was faring.

In January 1669, at Corinne's request, I painted a portrait of her, reclining on a sofa in her parlour, her bodice opened so that both her breasts were revealed. I took great care mixing colours on my palette to achieve the exact shades I wanted. For her fair complexion I used plenty of white, a touch of yellow and a little cadmium red and gave careful attention to the tones of highlights and shadows. I was certainly pleased with my representation of her ivory flesh and the impish gleam in her bright blue eyes, yet the vital essence of her beauty seemed to have eluded me. I was tempted to strive further, but I knew from past experience that if I persisted, I would run a grave risk of losing some of what I had already achieved. Corinne was clearly delighted with the completed work, and I suppose it was perhaps the best I had ever done.

During the five months between the end of October 1668 and the beginning of April 1669, I sometimes accompanied Corinne to the horse-racing on Newmarket Heath, which I found pleasant, even exciting, but I was not at all happy on the occasions I escorted her to society balls. I felt that my dancing was awkward and lacking in grace during the grand procession of the Pavane, the circling of the Bransle, the quick stepping of the Coranto or the Galliard and the group squares and rounds of the Country Dance. Corinne, however, seemed oblivious to my discomfort, enjoying every dance and openly flirting with other partners; she would gaily hum the tunes *Come Kiss Me Now*, *Cuckolds All Awry* or *Maiden Lane* all the way home in her private carriage.

Was I ever jealous and upset by Corinne's outrageous flirting and the many attentions paid to her by other young gallants? Indeed I was, dear readers. I was consumed with jealousy of every man she danced with and suffered actual pains in my abdomen when she permitted any of them to kiss her, as was the custom while dancing the Pavane or the Bransle. In fact, it would be true to say that I was jealous of every man who even looked at her. But, true to my nature, I never expressed my feelings on these matters to her. Conversely, never once did Corinne reproach me for my terpsichorean failings or, indeed, for any of my faults. In addition to being beautiful, vivacious and an arrant flirt, she was also generous and kind and accepted me exactly as I was. As Darby Malvor had once said to me, she was 'an absolute gem'.

Of course, I knew that on the days she was not with me, she often attended social functions in the company of her wide circle of friends and acquaintances, male as well as female. I tried not to dwell on the possible implications of this, because the pain of doing so was liable to keep me awake at night, close to tears. Yet, despite the anguish I suffered, I was, and remain, eternally grateful for our time together which, with the sole exception of those blissful hours with Harriet on the moonlit beach to the north-west of Riohacha, had been the only period in my life when I knew spells of true happiness.

One of Corinne's greatest delights was attending the theatre, which I also enjoyed, though not to the same extent. This introductory chapter now being completed, I shall commence the story of my further fortunes and misfortunes by relating one such visit to the theatre, which I had no reason to suspect would be the prelude to directing my life once more along the road of sorrow, sin and harrowing adventure.

2

Theatrical performances had been banned by the Puritans during the Commonwealth period, as were sports and other amusements, but the Restoration of King Charles II in 1660 had ushered in an outpouring of joyful activities. Old theatres were re-opened and new ones constructed, particularly in London.

The King's Theatre – also known as The Theatre Royal, The Covent Garden Theatre, The Drury Lane Theatre or Old Drury – was built in Brydges Street, just west of Drury Lane, only a short distance from the fashionable Covent Garden and with fairly easy access from the grand thoroughfare of The Strand. From its opening in May 1663, this theatre became famed for its spectacular scenery and fine productions of both tragedies and comedies, performed before audiences of at least seven hundred people.

On that balmy afternoon of Friday, 9 April 1669, Corinne and I had taken our seats in good time for the habitual three o'clock commencement of the performance. The interior of the moderately-sized auditorium was constructed almost entirely of wood, surmounted by a glazed cupola which was inclined to leak in wet weather. The first tier of boxes, with richly embroidered coverings, was raised only slightly above the pit and extended on both sides of the stage. These boxes, having an admission price of four shillings, were normally occupied by nobility, other privileged people, and sometimes royalty. As the widow of Sir Frederick Malvor, Corinne would certainly have qualified for a place in this tier, but preferred that we sit in one of the higher, adjoining boxes which constituted the middle gallery. Above us was the upper – and noisiest – gallery, where seats cost just one shilling.

Our own seats were priced at one shilling and sixpence and were comfortable enough, having coverings of green baize and gilt leather, as had the ascending rows of benches in the pit below us, where entry was two shillings and sixpence. These benches were filled with young gallants, flamboyantly dressed and sometimes the worse for drink; young ladies also in fine array and women of the town, peeping from behind their vizard masks.

In the passageway in front of the pit seats stood the orange-girls, their backs to the stage. They were dressed in coarse linen gowns and white smocks, with handkerchiefs around their necks, and held baskets of fruit covered with vine leaves. Their cries of, 'Oranges! Will you have any oranges?' rose repeatedly above the general hubbub, while the young gallants in the pit shouted witty and often indelicate comments in return but were nonetheless willing to purchase sweet China oranges at six pence apiece.

I was dressed that day in my favourite dove-grey, deep cuffed, velvet coat, dark-grey, broad-brimmed, ostrich-plumed hat, light-grey full breeches gathered into ribbon bands at my knees, silk stockings and high-tongued leather shoes. Perhaps I was not as richly clad as many of the audience in the boxes of the middle gallery – mostly merchants, goldsmiths and other such persons of wealth, usually accompanied by their finely attired wives or mistresses – but I paid little heed to any of them. As always, I could hardly take my eyes off Corinne as she gleefully watched the antics in the pit below.

On this occasion, she wore a full-sleeved, white silk gown, the low neckline of the pointed bodice cut square and adorned with silver lace and pale blue ribbon bows.

10

Round her neck was displayed the three-row pearl necklace I had given her, while a single string of pearls was wound around the top-knot of hair on the crown of her head. Her multitude of blonde ringlets flowed down to her creamy white shoulders and her breasts bulged tantalisingly above the upper edge of her bodice. She turned her head towards me now, her perfectly sculptured face whitened with ceruse, except where the cheeks were flushed by cochineal. Her bright blue eyes and smiling red lips conveyed how much she was enjoying herself.

'I liked to sit down in the pit once upon a time,' she confided in her refined but lively voice. 'But now I prefer merely to be an observer and pay more attention to the play.'

'I'm sure the players would be most gratified to know that there *are* people who come here to watch the play,' I replied.

Corinne reached over and squeezed my hand. 'I really want you to enjoy today, Nathaniel darling,' she said affectionately.

'Why today particularly?'

She looked away for a moment and then answered, 'Well, you delivered your manuscript to your publisher this morning, didn't you? And don't forget it's your birthday tomorrow. So you should be celebrating.'

'Yes, I suppose so,' I said, not totally convinced by her explanation.

At that moment, the flutes, hautboys and violins began to play from the music-room in a recess beneath the stage, and the curtain rose presently for the prologue. The wide stage extended considerably in front of the curtain and was illuminated by wax candles fixed upon sconces at both sides and chandeliers suspended from the proscenium arch. Brightly painted scenery, positioned in grooves at different depths upstage, provided an elaborate and colourful representation of the grounds of the Sicilian Court. The comedy being performed was yet another revival of *The Maiden Queen* by John Dryden, first aired in 1667, Nell Gwynne once more playing Florimel, maid of honour to the Queen of Sicily, and Charles Hart the courtier, Celadon.

Nell – former orange-girl and now the King's mistress – was making her first stage appearance for a few months, before playing Valeria in Dryden's new play, *Tyrannic Love*, to be staged the following week. With her gold-streaked bronze-red hair, mischievous hazel eyes, full bosom and lithe and provocative movements she looked ravishing. Seldom off the stage throughout the five long acts, she played her part with a saucy freshness that was consistently captivating, and a vitality and sparkle which never faded.

Corinne shrieked with laughter, as did most of the audience, as Nell delivered her lively lines and impromptu indelicate remarks. I found the dialogue decidedly witty, but rarely laughed aloud, though I greatly enjoyed it. Unfortunately, I was periodically distracted by the frequent disturbances down in the pit, caused by drunken, jesting gallants wandering about the narrow passageways between the benches and occasionally scuffling with one another in their endeavours to gain the favour of a particular lady. On the other hand, I experienced additional pleasure whenever Corinne ardently clasped my hand to her bosom under the cover of her delicately painted fan.

When Nell, disguised as a boy, danced a jig during the fifth act, thereby displaying her shapely legs, the only sound to be heard from the pit and the galleries was thunderous applause, which was repeated and prolonged when the much loved and good-humoured Nell took her final bow before the curtain came down.

Still smiling from her appreciation of the entertainment, Corinne now donned her lilac velvet hat, which had large white feathers curled along its wide brim, her silk mantle (also lilac) and her laced and perfumed gloves. In a flow of chattering people, we made our way down the short staircase into the thronged entrance hall. Here, we were suddenly confronted by a gentleman in his late fifties, wearing a dark brown periwig and a sky blue satin coat, decorated with silver buttons, a profusion of ribbons at the shoulders and enormous lace ruffles around the cuffs. He had a drooping, greyish moustache and a small tuft of beard on his chin. His eyes gleamed as, without hesitation, he put an arm around Corinne and gave her a firm kiss upon the lips.

I knew who he was – Thomas Killigrew, dramatist and manager of both the theatre and the King's Company of players. And, as I also knew his reputation as a rake, I was not greatly surprised, although certainly irritated, by his overfriendly greeting of Corinne. But so many men seemed to be on such familiar terms with her.

Killigrew now held both her hands and declared, 'Oh, sweet Corinne, what a vision of heavenly beauty you present to my eyes. Did you enjoy our play? Didn't you just love the pledges Florimel and Celadon made to one another that when they marry, they will respect each others' liberties to stray with other lovers? Wouldn't you say that perfectly described the marriage you wished you could have had with dear Sir Frederick?'

'That's very naughty, Tom,' Corinne replied in mock scolding tones. 'Now please behave yourself.'

Killigrew now looked towards me, releasing Corinne's hands.

'And who is this young gentleman?'

'This is Nathaniel Devarre, a portrait painter who was once a pirate,' Corinne proclaimed brightly.

She always seemed to take pleasure in introducing me as such to her friends.

'Come now, Corinne, you surely jest,' Killigrew scoffed. 'He certainly doesn't look like a pickaroon.'

I recognised the derivative from the Spanish word for rogue, *picarón*. He held out his hand to me.

'Thomas Killigrew. A pleasure to meet a friend of my one-time supper companion, the delightful Lady Malvor.'

I shook his hand and forced myself to reply pleasantly.

'Pleased to meet you, Mr Killigrew.'

He briefly perused me, shaking his head.

'Were you really a terror of the seas, throwing people to the sharks and deflowering young maidens?'

'I didn't do things like that,' I answered with some annoyance.

'Is that all you can say?' he asked scornfully. 'Can't you respond with some witty repartee?'

Before I could reply, he had turned to Corinne.

'What a dull young fellow you have found for yourself this time, Corinne. I hope he's livelier in bed.'

With a sudden upsurge of anger, I exclaimed, 'I'll be lively enough to thrust a rapier through your gizzard if you'd care to meet me on the field of honour.'

Corinne grasped my arm.

'Now, now, Nathaniel, we don't want any of that.'

'We don't indeed,' declared Killigrew with a broad grin. 'The field of honour? Good heavens, I'm far too old and out of practice for that. Anyway, when are you young gallants going to accept that duelling is now forbidden by law?'

He paused briefly, then added in sincere tones, 'I'm sorry if I offended you, young sir. I was being my usual tactless self. Forgive me.'

After firmly patting my arm, he turned to Corinne and kissed her hand.

'My fondest devotion will ever be with you, my sweet Corinne.'

With that, he turned and hastened over to a group of five gentlemen standing nearby, all of whom were merry with drink. They gave immediate voice to a song Killigrew had composed:

> Did you ever hear the like?
> Did you ever hear the fame?
> Of the five women barbers
> Who lived in Drury Lane?

Corinne fondly kissed my cheek and took my arm.

'Come on, darling,' she said. 'Let's be on our way.'

I was feeling rather foolish now, so said nothing as we descended the steps beneath the arched stone entranceway onto the cobbled street. Corinne's two-horse carriage promptly drew up in front of us from a line of similar conveyances. Coachmen, footmen and others attending their masters and mistresses, were always admitted free to the upper gallery once the curtain had risen for the final act, and could thereby know when the performance was ending and hasten to their expected duties. Dressed in dark blue livery, a footman opened the carriage door for us and I assisted Corinne to climb inside.

Soon we were on our way, the horses moving at a slow trot behind other carriages and sedan chairs, forcing carts and barrows into side alleys. The leather flaps to the window spaces were tied up, so that I could plainly see a few fruit stalls at the side of the road and more than a few attractive young girls employed as decoys by the notorious Madam Ross, Lady Du Lake and other brothel-keepers to lure young gallants, leaving the theatre, into visiting houses of ill repute in Lewkenor's Lane, Coalyard Alley or other slum byways off Drury Lane.

Sitting at my side, Corinne now took my hand.

'That was the first time I've ever seen you really angry,

Nathaniel,' she said. 'You gave me an awful shock. What on earth came over you?'

'I don't know. I was surprised myself,' I replied. 'All of a sudden, previously suppressed resentments just came to the surface and erupted.'

'What resentments?'

'The way all the men you know seem to feel free to lay hands on you, and I get fed up with people telling me I don't look like someone who could have been a pirate. I *was* a pirate, or at least a buccaneer, and I turned out to be a good one too. I've lived through horrific experiences that most of these scoffing fops couldn't even begin to comprehend.'

'You made my blood run cold. Memories of that terrible night when you killed Darby flashed through my mind. And what if Tom had accepted your challenge and you were to kill *him*? He has the King's favour. You could have been in no end of trouble.'

'I know, Corinne,' I said with a sigh. 'I acted foolishly back there. I realise that now. I'm usually a cautious person, even under provocation, but very occasionally I have these rash impulses which are inclined to over-rule my common sense.'

Our carriage now turned right into The Strand, heading towards Charing Cross, Pall Mall and eventually St James's Square.

Corinne squeezed my hand. 'Well, let's forget all that. I so much want us to enjoy ourselves, Nathaniel. We've never yet had a quarrel, have we? So let's not have one now.'

'No, let's not,' I said with a smile.

3

The Malvor mansion, situated on the northern side of St James's Square, had become a second home to me. While residing there for two or three days each week, I had grown very fond of the place, gradually giving less thought to the dark memories its principal staircase had the power to evoke.

Corinne's steward, Matheson, was a former soldier who, in common with most of the people of England, hated Catholics. He was consequently well disposed towards me since learning that I had fought the Spanish. Quite frequently, he would greet me with, 'Good afternoon, Mr Devarre. Been killing any more papists lately?' Although somewhat irritated by this, I was always careful never to show my annoyance, as I had good reason to wish to maintain Matheson's favour. Anyway, I generally liked the man. On the other hand, the firm and solemn housekeeper, Mrs Bradrock, was coolly polite to me on all occasions. But I gathered that she had always disapproved of all of Corinne's gentlemen friends, whom by some unfathomable logic she held responsible for her mistress's sinful conduct, without attaching any blame to her Ladyship herself.

The largest room in the mansion was the dining hall, the main windows of which opened onto the terrace, beyond which lay an extensive garden. The walls of this room were hung with tapestries of rural scenes, and the polished oak dining table was flanked by chairs upholstered in red velvet, decorated with silver lace.

Corinne and I took our usual places at opposite ends

of this table when we sat down to supper just after seven o'clock that night. The cook-maid placed bowls and platters containing pease pottage, prawns, lobsters, tongue pie, sweet potato and burdock tart, within our immediate reach, from which we helped ourselves. The cutlery was all of engraved silver and included the still novel two-pronged forks the King had introduced into England from France upon his Restoration in 1660.

Taking a sip from my silver wine-cup, I found the taste of its contents pleasant but not at all familiar. Corinne's wine cellar was well stocked with wines from Bordeaux, Burgundy, Florence, the Rhine Valley and even from the Levant and the Greek Islands, and I had regularly enjoyed them all, but this one was definitely new to me. I glanced again at the plain label hung around the neck of the bottle. It merely said: PARIS WINE.

'Paris wine?' I said now to Corinne. 'What does that mean?'

Corinne smiled and replied eagerly, 'Apparently, it's produced from vineyards flourishing on the slopes of Montmartre. I obtained a dozen bottles from James Houblon, the merchant adventurer of Winchester Street. It's rather nice, don't you think?'

'Yes, it is,' I said and took another sip. 'You're always full of surprises, Corinne. I never tasted the luscious Malmsey until I dined with you.'

The habitual zest of Corinne's bright and lively blue eyes now yielded to concern as she spoke with unusual seriousness.

'You have been happy during your time with me, haven't you, Nathaniel?'

I had a vague suspicion that something was not quite right. Both in the theatre and in the carriage coming home she had emphasised that she wanted us to enjoy today, and now she was asking me this. But I was often inclined to become anxious about things when there proved to be no need.

'Of course I have,' I replied. 'You've given me the happiest period of my entire life, and long may it continue.'

Corinne now raised her wine-cup.

'Here's to us, my dear Nathaniel,' she said with considerable feeling.

'To us.'

As I raised my own cup, I thought once more how beautiful and warm-hearted she was and how much I wished she could love me as I loved her. This was the one thing I dearly craved – something I had always been denied – the joy of being mutually in love.

Having finished my helping of tongue pie, I now served myself a portion of tart. In an attempt to shrug off my anxieties and longings, I decided to change the subject.

'I've noticed Sir Frederick's library contains a quantity of religious volumes with an anti-Rome bias: *The Sincere Convert, The Saints' Everlasting Rest, The Call to the Unconverted* and other such writings.'

'Oh yes,' Corinne exclaimed, back to her exuberant self. 'Stuffy old Frederick used to read all that boring drivel.' She laughed gently. 'All I read are twopenny stories of romance and murder.'

'But you are a believer?' I queried.

'Of course. You know I am. I attend church every Sunday, but that's enough for me.'

She paused for a moment, then said, 'I'm inclined to forget that you're pretty devout. I hope I didn't upset you by calling Frederick's books drivel.'

'Not at all,' I replied. 'Your husband's books don't reflect my viewpoint anyway. At the moment, I'm halfway through reading *The Life and Death of the Holy Jesus* by Jeremy Taylor. That's more to my taste.'

After drinking some more wine, I said, 'I know you

only married Sir Frederick for his wealth and title. You told me so yourself once. What about *his* intention? Was he very disappointed when you never provided him with an heir?'

'He certainly was. He used to call me a barren bitch and all sorts.' She laughed gaily. 'But he loved me just the same in his own possessive way. I have to give him that, the pompous old trout!'

She laughed again. I marvelled at the fact that it never seemed to have bothered her in the least that I had killed her husband in a duel, and it had only temporarily disturbed her when I killed her brother-in-law and lover, Darby. But both killings continued to be of considerable concern to me, particularly the second. Even though I now preferred to believe in the loving and merciful God that Harriet Abercorn had spoken of, rather than the severe and vengeful deity my father had taught me to fear, I considered the chances of my own salvation pretty remote.

'What about that young girl you hoped to marry? Have you heard any more of her?'

'No, not since she left the village.'

'Have you any regrets about not accepting her father's offer?'

'Oh yes, I've often regretted it, but in the end I've always reached the same conclusion. I was right to decline the offer. Mary had a strong aversion to me at first, and although she eventually accepted that I was basically a good person, she still abhorred the idea of having an intimate relationship with me.'

'Never mind, Nathaniel,' Corinne said with a sympathetic smile. 'You'll find someone else.'

'I've already found someone else,' I declared. 'I love you every bit as much as I love Mary – if not more.'

'Oh, darling Nathaniel, I'm very flattered by your devotion to me, but you should really find someone to marry.'

My heart increased its beat as I said, 'Perhaps you are that person, Corinne.'

Looking rather flustered now, Corinne exclaimed, 'Oh, do stop talking nonsense! Come on, drink the rest of your wine and we'll return to the parlour.'

The walls of her cozy parlour were hung with blue silk panels; green velvet curtains were drawn across the windows. We sat in elbow chairs, covered with purple figured satin, at a small round table. By the light of many branched candelabra, we played several hands of our own version of the complicated card game, ombre, intended for three players when played correctly. As always, we wagered shillings and caught each other cheating, the hilarity this occasioned being encouraged by a bottle of Canary sack. In between hands, we would raise our conical glasses and sing together:

> Sack will the soul of poetry infuse,
> Be that my theme and muse.

And so it was that we were in a merry mood when we retired early to bed, after a nightcap of posset – a delicious hot mixture of eggs, sack, sugar, nutmeg and cream infused with cinnamon, reputed to be an aphrodisiac; not that either of us required any such stimulus.

What can I say of Corinne's bedchamber with its garish décor of purple silk hung panels, red and orange woollen rugs and blue curtains, embroidered in gold, around the four-poster bed, its orange velvet coverlet trimmed with gold braid? And what can I say of Corinne as she disrobed herself of her white silk gown, her petticoat trimmed with gold lace, her knitted garters and her lilac silk stockings? Indeed, what can I say about when she lay back upon the bed, her luxuriant blonde tresses flowing over the pillow, her naked beauty glowing in the candlelight and her eyes as warm and inviting as her slender arms reaching out eagerly to embrace me?

I am sorry, dear readers, but I have no intention of saying anything about any of these things, but will instead move on to the following day.

On that fine spring morning, Corinne and I ate breakfast, seated side by side at a wicker table upon the terrace. As always, I greatly appreciated the clear outlook over the garden, bisected by a broad, gravel path extending from the terrace to the boundary wall. Narrow paths further divided the square flower-beds, which were planted with tulips and polyanthus. I must say it was decidedly pleasant sitting there, consuming our oysters, bread, cream and small ale.

Corinne sat on my left, clad in a loose silk negligée, while I was similarly at ease in my linen shirt and breeches. Although Corinne was strangely quiet, I felt so happy and content, if a little weary from insufficient sleep, that I thought little of it until she took another mouthful of small ale and spoke.

'Nathaniel dear, there's something I have to say to you and there's no point in my putting it off any longer. The reason I said yesterday that I wanted you particularly to enjoy being with me was because this will be our last time together.'

It was as though my heart had stopped. I felt an actual jolt in my chest and experienced a chill tremor. With incredulity, I turned my head and stared at her, unable to speak.

'You see, I haven't got much time left.'

'Why?' I asked in a quavering tone. 'Are you – are you dying?'

Corinne laughed. 'Of course I'm not dying, you silly boy. I meant I haven't much time left in which to remarry.'

'But you could marry me whenever you like.'

'Oh, dear Nathaniel,' she said, patting my forearm, 'I couldn't possibly marry a portrait painter of middling social status. I need a husband of considerable wealth and, if possible, with a title. Even though I am reasonably well off at the moment, funds are gradually dwindling. Frederick was a heavy gambler and squandered much of his inheritance, and the incomes in rents and sales from his estates around Tavistock are not always satisfactory and usually in arrears. I have to start making some provision for my future.'

I looked down at the table now, my mind in great consternation.

'Do we really have to part so soon?' I asked.

'Yes, Nathaniel, I'm afraid we do. You must understand my position. Time is against me as far as the marriage market is concerned. Most men are seeking young virgin brides with large dowries. I would come with a reasonable dowry, but the only other thing I have in my favour is my beauty. And how much longer will that last? I shall be thirty-two next month. Every night I bathe my face with a fine cloth soaked in myrrh water, hoping to keep the wrinkles at bay, and my physician calls once a month to bleed me from a vein and give me a stimulant of chalybeate water and a purging potion, but how long can these measures prevail against advancing years? And remember my reputation. Thomas Killigrew once told me that I'm known in Whitehall as "the Dishonourable Lady Trollop of St James's Square".'

'Yes,' I said. 'Lord Abercorn once described you to me in similar terms.'

'Exactly,' Corinne said with a shrug. 'Oh, I'm very popular just the same – with men, though not usually with their spouses. But as a prospective wife I don't rate highly at all. Even so, there are possibilities amongst the upper strata that I can work on.'

'What kind of possibilities?' I enquired, dreading the answer.

'Oh, perhaps some wealthy widower in his dotage, or some innocent youth, obsessed with his mother and easily attracted to older women, or even someone so addicted to drink that his mind is constantly befuddled.'

'So you'd rather have someone like that than me,' I said sourly.

'Oh darling, of course I wouldn't. If you had pots of money I would marry you in an instant. You're the only man I've ever known with whom I've been able to live in complete harmony. But you haven't got pots of money and never will have. So I have no choice but to seek a husband elsewhere. That's why we've just got to separate, Nathaniel. I can no longer be known to be sleeping with a portrait painter or anyone else. I have to begin creating a reformed image without delay. It's not going to be easy. It might take me months – maybe a year – to ensnare some suitably wealthy person, but I need to make a start now. So we must say goodbye. You can understand that, can't you, Nathaniel?'

I bowed my head, overcome by sadness, and was unable to suppress a sob. Corinne instantly reached out to me with both arms and cradled my head upon her bosom.

'Oh dear, dear darling,' she said tenderly. 'Oh, you mustn't be like this.'

I pulled free from her grasp and rose to my feet.

'I'm sorry, I have to go,' I said hastily, blinking back my tears.

'Nathaniel, please stay till after dinner,' Corinne pleaded urgently. 'We can go back up to bed if you like. After all, it's your birthday.'

'No.' I shook my head. 'If we must part, then it has to be now. I'll always be grateful for what we've had, Corinne. But I wanted it forever, and if I can't have that ... Oh my God! I've got to go.'

I turned and hastened away through the dining hall, my numbed mind hardly conscious of my surroundings. Somehow, I managed to collect my hat and coat and departed from the mansion into St James's Square. I suppose the sun must have been shining but I did not notice. It seemed to me my whole existence had descended into darkness.

It was only when the coach was passing through the village of Islington, on the road north to Highgate, that I remembered I had left the gold watch Corinne had given me for my birthday on the bedside table.

4

The gathering clouds matched my sombre mood as I exited beneath the large lantern overhanging the portal of the White Hart Inn on that overcast April afternoon. Three tankards of Old Hun ale had produced a degree of calm but had not lifted me out of my depression. Pausing to button my knee-length coat, I glanced across at the ornate iron gates of the Parkfield mansion. Then, turning right along the earthen road, I shortly passed Arundel House, built in the Tudor style with projecting upper walls and spacious windows. Beyond the village green to the left of the road, the tall towers and chimneys of Dorchester House were prominent, as was the adjacent row of stately trees. On the border of the bowling green stood my own modest stone house behind its hedge of briar roses. Before crossing the top of the narrow Swine's Lane, I had to pass the two fenced ponds on my left, which stretched across the village green towards the Gatehouse Tavern at the top. Beyond the bottom pond, beside a burgeoning elm tree, stood the stone and timber forge. Thomas Sconce, the blacksmith, looked up from his anvil and bade me a cheery good day. I responded as heartily as I could before entering the ancient Angel Inn, opposite the forge.

The oak wainscoting of the taproom bore little decoration beyond a few dull paintings of village life hung between the windows of the wall facing Holloway Hill. A serving wench was within the door as I entered and greeted me with some surprise.

'Good day, Mr Devarre. I didn't expect to see you 'ere at this time of the day. Alderman Byde's?'

'Please, Lucinda,' I answered.

I took a seat at a table in an alcove adjacent to the entrance door, while Lucinda made her way behind the bar, saying something to the proprietor, William Fisher, which I was unable to hear. There were only a few customers in the taproom but the smell of Virginia tobacco from their clay pipes was, nonetheless, strong. The fact that I never partook of tobacco was considered by most of the residents of Highgate to be another of my eccentricities.

Lucinda returned shortly and placed a pewter tankard of Alderman Byde's ale before me, for which I paid her a penny.

'Thank you kindly, Mr Devarre. I thought you always went to the Gatehouse at midday.'

I looked up at her now. Her dark hair spiralled untidily down to the bulging bodice of her cotton gown. She was a rather comely lass, if somewhat pale in countenance.

'Normally I do,' I replied. 'But Jeremy Grenville and Timothy Cottle are almost sure to be in there, and I don't feel like company today.'

I took a sip from my tankard. Alderman Byde's was my favourite ale.

'Jeremy never comes in 'ere now,' Lucinda said sadly. I 'aven't seen 'im for weeks.'

I nodded but made no comment.

'D'you 'ave any idea why, Mr Devarre?'

Perhaps I should have pleaded ignorance, but it seemed to me she was entitled to an explanation.

'I believe his wife was growing suspicious,' I said with a slight shrug.

'Then why 'asn't 'e told me that 'iself? I may be just a common serving wench to 'im, but I've got feelings just as much as 'is fancy wife 'as.'

27

Tears formed in her eyes as she added sadly, 'Love is very cruel, Mr Devarre.'

'I'll give you no argument there, Lucinda,' I declared. 'If I thought I was going to fall in love tomorrow, I would kill myself tonight. Never again would I wish to suffer the destructive torment of that accursed affliction.'

'Oh, Mr Devarre!' she exclaimed with concern. 'You wouldn't really do yourself in, would you? Why d'you say such a thing?'

I drank a mouthful of ale, surprised at her evident distress over my rather foolish remark.

'Oh, there are reasons, Lucinda,' I said. 'Believe me, there are reasons.'

'Lucinda!' William Fisher called out. 'There are other customers to serve, girl.'

She hastened away. I drank some more ale and pondered over my present state of mind and my utterances to Lucinda.

Four days had now passed since Corinne had broken my heart – to use a well worn but very apt phrase. During those days I had ventured only as far as the market to buy food – not that I had had much of an appetite. The rest of the daylight hours I had spent within my studio on the upper floor of my house, quaffing copious amounts of wine and subjecting a canvas to layers of frantically applied paint as I desperately endeavoured to capture the essence of Corinne's beauty from memory. Needless to say, I did not succeed. On the contrary, the results were grotesque, and after four drunken, frenzied days, I found myself so frustrated and angered by my failures as both painter and lover that I carved and ripped the canvas into pieces, swearing never to pick up a paint brush again.

Every night during this period, my fitful sleep had been disturbed by nightmares that encompassed all my past

28

ordeals: my father leaning over me, his eyes burning with fervour and his podgy finger wagging as he ranted and raved; the Dutch fireships bearing down upon the *Invincible* off the coast of Flanders, while my terror-stricken brain struggled to function; blood spurting from Captain Kincaid's chest as he fell dying upon the quarterdeck of the Spanish galleon in the mouth of the Rio de la Hacha; Harriet's bones scattered upon the river bank; Mary's stately beauty and withering disdain. Interspersed with all of these images was Corinne, smiling at me provocatively while hands of unseen men wandered all over her body. And whenever I jolted awake in the early hours, fiery demons came screaming at me out of the darkness. Perhaps I was still dreaming, but I believed myself awake and consequently lay in bed petrified for several minutes after their departure.

So it was that after I had destroyed the hopelessly painted canvas that morning, I at last washed and shaved, splashing my lower face with orange-flower water, dined frugally on cold pigeon pie, cheesecake and small ale, cleaned my teeth with utilitarian powder on my brisk finger and dressed in fresh clothing. Then, seeking some relief from my severe depression, I had set out on this drinking spree, starting at the White Hart Inn and continuing now in the preferred Angel Inn.

My ruminations were shortly disturbed by four middle-aged gentlemen, seated at a table by the brick fireplace, who suddenly burst into song.

> Skip it and trip it nimbly, nimbly.
> Tickle it, tickle it lustily.
> Strike up the tabor for the wenches' favour.
> Tickle it, tickle it lustily.

Quite inexplicably I began to sing myself.

If few there be amongst us, our hearts are very
   great.
And each'll have more plunder, and each'll have
   more plate...

I broke off, suddenly aware that all four gentlemen had
turned their heads and were glowering in disapproval at
my untimely interruption of their harmonious rendering.

I raised my tankard in salutation and called over, 'My
apologies, gentlemen. Pray continue.'

They looked fleetingly from one to another, then gave
hearty voice to the second verse.

Let us be seen on Highgate Green,
To dance for the honour of Holloway.
Since we are come hither, let's spare for no leather,
To dance for the honour of Holloway.

I paid little heed to their singing, however, as my mind
sought an explanation for my interruption. Why had I
begun to sing that pirate ditty? It had seemed to burst
from my inner soul unbidden. After pondering for only
a few moments, a message clearly came to me, I believed,
from my guardian angel. I was being shown a way to cure
my present heartache.

Hadn't Corinne said that creating a reformed image
and ensnaring a wealthy husband, considering her age
and reputation, might take a year? And hadn't she also
declared that if only I had pots of money, she would
marry me in an instant? Well then – what was the one
place where such a fortune could readily be obtained? It
was obvious. The Spanish Main! I must return to the New
World and help myself to a vast amount of Spanish gold
and silver.

During the last few days I had once more been castigating

30

myself for my failures in life. But what was the one rôle in which I had not been a failure? That of buccaneer! It could not be denied that the raid on Riohacha had ended in disaster and I had returned to England with only one pearl necklace to show for all the hazards and ordeals I had endured. But that had been the consequence of ill fortune and did not reflect upon my own performance in that piratical venture. Had not members of my crew assured me I was the best captain they'd ever served under, apart from Captain Kincaid? Surely I had no reason to doubt my ability to obtain substantial plunder, and why shouldn't fortune smile upon me for once?

'By the Devil's hoof!' I ecstatically exclaimed.

The four gentlemen by the fireplace looked round at me once more, and William Fisher and Lucinda also glanced across from the bar.

Fisher enquired, 'Do you wish another ale, Mr Devarre?'

'No thank you, Mr Fisher,' I replied. 'I've got to say some prayers.'

With that, I drained my tankard and made for the door, ignoring the six pairs of startled eyes which watched my exit.

Once outside, I directed my steps towards the top of Holloway Hill, passing the blacksmith's forge, an alehouse, a cluster of cottages and a few strolling villagers who either ignored me or greeted me perfunctorily. Just past South Wood Lane, I stepped aside to allow passage of a horse-drawn cart, loaded with agricultural produce, which had just driven cautiously through the narrow toll gate. On reaching this arched gateway at the junction with Caen Wood Lane and the Toll Road, I turned to my right and entered Highgate Chapel, adjacent to Sir Roger Cholmeley's Bequest School for poor boys.

The chapel's preacher, William Ruthband, had come here after being deprived of his Presbyterian Ministry in

Essex by the Act of Uniformity. Apart from the Quaker Meeting house in South Wood Lane, the chapel was the only place of worship in the village, and Ruthband welcomed people of all denominations, except Catholics, to listen to his powerful sermons on Gospel truths. Although he was saddened by my conversion from Presbyterianism to Anglicanism, he treated me kindly, as part of his flock.

Alone in the chapel now, I faced the unadorned altar, void of any Christian symbol, made the sign of the cross, which I would never do during a service here, and thanked God for his revelation to me. In retrospect, I doubt if the Almighty would wish to be credited with my decision to return to piracy, but at that time I was convinced I had received divine guidance. I prayed that Corinne should not find a suitable husband before I had returned from my intended venture safe, sound and wealthy.

Spiritually renewed, and with strengthened resolve, I now left the chapel and walked happily across the road towards the entrance of the Gatehouse Tavern. It was going to be my pleasure to buy Jeremy Grenville and Timothy Cottle a drink or two in celebration of my imminent departure for Port Royal, Jamaica.

5

After a tedious nine-week voyage, during which rough seas rendered me horribly sick on two occasions, I eventually arrived in Port Royal in the late afternoon of Monday, 28 June 1669.

The town had grown during my eleven months' absence, both in size and prosperity. Five hundred houses were now crowded together on the long sandspit which curved south and then west from the southern coast of the island. Liberally distributed amongst these brick and timber dwellings were numerous taverns, grog shops, brothels and gaming houses. Sugar plantations were multiplying along the island's coastal plains and in the foothills of the towering, lush Blue Mountains, and the merchants of Port Royal were making fortunes by trading for pirate plunder and from contraband trade with the Spanish colonies. These colonies were especially in need of textiles, glass and paper, as well as Negro slaves who were being brought from West Africa in large numbers to work on Jamaica's plantations. There was also money to be made shipping sugar, indigo, cotton, tobacco, mahogany and dye-woods to England. As the extensive deep water harbour, lined with huge warehouses, could accommodate large numbers of vessels, Port Royal had quickly become the busiest and most prosperous trading centre in the Caribbean.

Buccaneers – who maintained with a modicum of justification that they were not pirates – were the guarantors of this prosperity and indeed of England's continued colonisation of Jamaica. It was only their presence that deterred the Spanish from launching an invasion to repossess the island, and it was the buccaneers who had maintained the continual flow into Port Royal of Spanish gold, silver, emeralds, pearls, silks, laces, brocades and religious treasures. A cannon fired from Fort Charles, guarding the narrow channel into the inlet, heralded the approach of the returning buccaneer vessels and immediately alerted government officials, creditors, merchants, tavern keepers and harlots to hasten to the harbour wharfs or otherwise prepare themselves to gather in a fresh harvest of wealth. It naturally followed that if I wished to acquire a personal fortune, this was the place to be – or so I reasoned.

Despite discomfort from the heat of the sun and worries about my personal safety, I also experienced considerable joy at being back in this den of wealth and wickedness. In a one-horse carriage, with a sullen yet respectful African driver, I proceeded immediately to the Sea Horse Tavern in Queen Street, arriving before six o'clock in the evening.

Wearing a dark green coat and plumed hat, and bearing my sea-chest on my shoulder, I crossed the timber porch and entered the wide-open doorway. Nothing had changed. In a stench of human sweat and Virginia and Spanish tobacco smoke, raucous seafaring men and lascivious whores, seated around the scattered tables, supped from their tankards and shouted, laughed and sang in a cacophony of uproar. And there, in front of the long bar, talking to her robust assistant manager, was Nancy.

Readers of my previous memoir will recall that Nancy was in her late twenties and had spent her adolescent years as a whore on the streets of Edinburgh. After grievously wounding a violent customer, she was deported to Barbados as a bondservant where she was purchased by a wealthy merchant. But when his wife discovered that this buxom Scottish wench was performing services for her husband far beyond those of a maid, Nancy was promptly shipped off to Jamaica. The merchant, however, having been greatly enamoured with Nancy, provided her with substantial funds which enabled her to buy the Sea Horse Tavern upon arrival in Port Royal. Since then, hunger and poverty had become a distant memory and her prosperity increased year by year.

I picked my way between the tables and approached unobserved. When I tapped her on the shoulder, she turned abruptly. For a moment she seemed perplexed, but then her face lit up.

'Nathaniel Devarre!' she exclaimed in her pleasant Scottish accent. 'Rip me if I ever expected tae see you again.'

My eyes swiftly took in her mass of auburn curls, her robust yet appealing features, her green eyes and her full-bosomed body, clad in a scarlet silk gown.

'Hello, Nancy,' I said, with a smile. 'It's a pleasure to see you again.'

'And you,' she replied enthusiastically, giving me a hefty thump on the chest. 'What in the name of all that's holy are you doing back in Port Royal? Rescuing another damsel in distress?'

'Something like that,' I answered evasively.

'Well, you can tell me all about it over supper. Come on, I'll find you a room upstairs and you can clean up and rest a wee while.'

I followed Nancy round the side of the bar and up the creaking, wooden staircase. In the dimly lit corridor at the top, she showed me into a barely furnished room with badly cracked walls. It was the one I had occupied on my previous visit.

'Home, sweet home,' I sighed, lowering my sea-chest to the plank floor.

'Well, it's no much, but what d'you expect at this price?' she laughed gently. 'I'll send you up some water and refreshment.'

She left. I took off my hat and coat and sat down upon the small bed, feeling suddenly weary.

Well, I'd got here safe and sound, I considered. That was the easy bit. But what exactly was I going to do next? I wanted to seize a fortune in Spanish gold, but how? Where would I start?

Then, in my mind, I saw Corinne lying upon her bed, her blonde tresses spread across the pillow, her blue eyes shining as she drew me down upon her delightful naked flesh. Such images had taunted me throughout the voyage from England. I *had* to get her back. I couldn't bear the prospect of a lifetime without her. Somehow, I would obtain that Spanish gold. By God, I would!

This determination partially restored my spirits, though I was still none the wiser as to how I should proceed. Shortly, there came a knock on the door and a Negro boy brought me in a wooden bucket of water and a tankard of beer. I flipped open the tankard's pewter lid and gratefully quenched my thirst, then lifted the bucket onto the small table and washed my face and upper body. There was no fresh water in Port Royal. Consequently, every morning, watermen in dozens of small boats had to ferry in supplies in wooden casks filled at the mouth of the River Cobre. The water was not, however, considered safe to drink.

Soon after seven o'clock I was summoned to Nancy's room. The walls here were much more presentable, having mahogany panelling, and the bed was a four-poster with orange and gold curtains. In one corner was a substantial money chest, next to a tall desk with what I presumed to be accounts ledgers piled up on it.

Seated opposite Nancy at the central table, I surveyed

the foodstuffs on the pewter platters. I filled my plate – also pewter – with turtle, buttered crabs and sweet-tasting manatee, and was glad to feed myself with my knife and fingers, for I had never adjusted to manipulating forks, as used by Corinne and some of her aristocratic friends.

'So tell me, Nathaniel,' began Nancy, 'what's your reason for returning tae Port Royal?'

I took a drink of the strong Madeira wine before replying.

'Quite simply, Nancy, I've come here to obtain gold and silver from the Spanish.'

'Then I'm afraid you've picked the wrong time tae come,' she answered. 'Just last Thursday, Governor Sir Thomas Modyford issued a proclamation throughout the island, emphasising the Crown's directive against anti-Spanish hostilities. Until further ordered, he said, the subjects of His Catholic Majesty of Spain are tae be treated as good neighbours and friends. So all privateering activities have been suspended. Any buccaneer who disregards the proclamation will be liable tae be hung.'

My jaw dropped. I could not believe my ill fortune, though it but reflected the pattern of my life hitherto.

Nancy continued, 'Apparently, the English Secretary of State reminded Modyford of this while Henry Morgan was busy sacking Maracaibo. The buccaneer fleet got back here a month ago, loaded with plunder, and now they canny sail again. The boys areny very pleased, I can tell you.'

'No, and neither am I,' I exclaimed, thumping the table with my fist. 'Of all the things to happen!'

'Well, it winny last long, you can be sure of that. If you hang about for a few months, the Spanish are sure tae resume their harassment and scheming tae recapture Jamaica, and Modyford will sanction the resumption of attacks tae keep the dagos in their place.'

I shook my head and continued eating as I spoke.

'I can't afford to hang about for a few months. I need to obtain a fortune to take back to London as soon as possible.'

Nancy almost choked on her mouthful of turtle and laughed derisively.

'You are insane, Nathaniel Devarre. Nobody comes back from a buccaneer raid with a personal share amounting tae a fortune; not even Admiral Morgan. If you took part in profitable ventures for a year or so and saved every penny of your shares, instead of squandering it all on rum, whoors and dice as all of them do, I suppose you might amass a *small* fortune – but no otherwise.'

I stared at her for a moment, recognising the patent absurdity of my desperate mission. Nonetheless, I answered defiantly.

'I don't care what you say, Nancy. I'm going to get a fortune. I've got to – and quickly. With all the gold, silver, emeralds and pearls that are out there on the Spanish Main, there must be a way of doing it.'

She picked up the onion-shaped bottle and refilled both of our silver wine-cups.

'Well, dinny look tae me for a solution. It just isny possible.'

I now filled my plate with larded parrot and boiled onions.

'It must be possible,' I protested. 'Or my guardian angel wouldn't have sent me here.'

Nancy raised her eyebrows and smirked.

'Your guardian angel?'

'Yes. He directed me to return to the New World.'

'And where exactly did this happen?'

'In a tavern in my village, just outside London.'

'I didny ken angels frequented taverns.'

'Well, it *was* called the Angel Inn,' I pointed out jocularly.

'The notion came to me in a sudden revelation which could only have come from heaven.'

'It's more likely tae have come out of a tankard of ale,' Nancy declared. 'Tell me this, Nathaniel. Why do you have a need of so much money? And why is it so urgent?'

I took another mouthful of Madeira while considering how to explain it. The simple truth seemed best.

'I'm very much in love with a widow in London, Lady Corinne Malvor. She's seeking a rich husband to guarantee her future. So I have to obtain great wealth and return home before she marries someone else.'

'Oh, dearie me.' Nancy shook her head. 'What folly and disaster this love nonsense can cause. I've never felt like that about anyone. All I ever want from a man is a good fuck. I haveny any need for flowers and declarations of everlasting devotion.'

She drained her wine-cup and refilled both, while I piled some chopped onion on my last slice of parrot.

'Then you can count yourself lucky,' I said. 'I only wish I could be like that.'

Nancy had finished eating and she leaned forward against the table, giving me a fuller view of her magnificent breasts, bulging above the gold and silver laced neckline of her scarlet silk bodice so that I could all but see her nipples. The very sight of such fleshly splendour made me temporarily forget Corinne and I longed to avail myself of carnal delights closer at hand.

Looking up into Nancy's eyes now, I had almost forgotten what we were talking about, but her words soon cut through my lustful reverie.

'Some of the boys have already left for Tortuga, hoping tae continue plundering the Spanish under the protection of the French flag. You could do the same, but if you want maximum profit, you'd need tae be captain of a small vessel with minimum crew tae share the loot. Even then, I canny see you ever getting what you could call a fortune from your captain's share.'

'I suppose that would be my best option,' I said. 'But where am I going to get a small vessel?'

'I'll get one for you,' she replied. 'It so happens I ken the owner of a small sloop who is planning tae marry and settle ashore. I'm sure I can purchase it from him for a reasonable price.'

I was quite astounded by her generosity.

'Why would you do that for me, Nancy?'

'Look, Nathaniel, I haveny got a fortune, but I've got more money than I ken what tae do with and there's more coming in all the time. I can well afford tae buy a sloop, and I can always sell it again when you've finished with it. So I've nothing tae lose. And anyway, I really like you. I dinny ken why. You're no really my type of man.'

'Not like Captain Kincaid,' I commented sourly.

'Exactly. Jonathon was a real man in every way. Just the same, you're the nicest wee man I ever met, and I find your naïve idealism very refreshing in this sordid world. This scheme of yours is idiotic, yet you're determined tae pursue it. I admire you for that. So I'm going tae buy that sloop.'

First Nancy had made me feel bad about myself, and then surprisingly good. I was confused but happy as I sat back, my appetite now sated.

'Believe me, I am most grateful for your help and generosity.'

'Captain Lowther should be in the tavern later tonight, as is his custom. I'll bring him up here and do a deal with him.'

'Would it help if I were in attendance?'

'No, it wouldny. I'll negotiate better if I'm alone. I'll take him tae bed if he's willing tae lower his price.'

I felt my face flush as I experienced a jumble of emotions – anger, jealousy, disgust and resentment.

'You surely don't have to do that,' I said forcefully.

She stared at me for a moment before answering firmly, 'It winny be any penance. Lowther is my kind of man.'

'Like Jonathon Kincaid.'

'No quite, but he's got seductive eyes and a fair amount of charm.'

'I thought you said he was planning to marry.'

Nancy laughed. 'For God's sake, Nathaniel! The fact that he's getting married winny hold him back. What kind of puritanical fairyland do you live in?' She stood up. 'Now, off you go. I've got things tae do. I'll see you in the morning.'

Still feeling agitated, I got up and walked to the door, where I paused and managed to speak calmly.

'Thank you for supper, Nancy, and for your kindness.'

'Och, it's a pleasure, Nathaniel. And dinny worry. I'll get you that sloop.'

I nodded and left the room, forgetting to say goodnight.

6

Despite the humidity, mosquitoes and drunken revellers in the street below, I slept well that night and did not awaken until 9.30 the following morning, when Nancy entered my room without knocking. She was followed by the Negro boy, carrying a tray from which he deposited upon the table platters of oysters, plantains and cassava bread, plus a tankard of beer. Nancy then cheerily instructed me to get up and get dressed, as she wished to show me the sloop she now owned.

Consequently, within an hour, I was travelling with Nancy in her red and gold carriage, drawn by two white horses, down bustling Queen Street to the junction with Lime Street, and then via an alleyway to Fisher's Row. Here we turned left, passing numerous waterfront taverns and drinking dens which were not short of customers, even this early in the day. Soon we reached the sheltered cove known as Chocolata Hole. Perhaps a hundred sloops, ketches and other shallow draft boats were either anchored or moored here, larger vessels being accommodated in the deep water harbour on the northern shore, bordering Thames Street.

Alighting from the carriage, we walked across the wooden wharf. This morning, Nancy was wearing a pink satin gown, embroidered with silver lace, and a red velvet hat with large white plumes along the brim. As always, she exuded sensuality.

'Here we are, Nathaniel,' she said with great satisfaction. 'This is your new ship, the *Lady Bess.*'

We halted. Moored to the wharf before me lay a Bermuda

sloop, which I later established to be 35 feet in length with a displacement of thirty tons. She had a hull of cedar planking, bounded by two parallel white timber wales, and a single fore-and-aft rigged mast fitted at a rakish angle, sloping slightly aft. The long bowsprit added to its aggressive appearance. The larboard bulwark facing me was pierced with ports for three guns on the single deck. I was impressed.

'She looks good, Nancy,' I said. 'But with your permission, I shall rename her the *Lady Corinne*.'

'How d'you ken I dinny want tae call her the *Mistress Nancy*?'

'Would you want to call her that?' I asked anxiously.

Nancy laughed. 'Of course I wouldny. You'll be the captain; so you call her what you like.'

'Right,' I said, relieved. 'Let's step aboard.'

I approached the boarding ladder, then paused.

'D'you want me to help you up?'

'D'you think I'm feeble or something?' she replied indignantly. 'I'm every bit as fit and strong as you are.'

'Sorry,' I muttered.

As I began to ascend the ladder, she called behind me, 'You're going tae get a nice wee surprise in a moment, Nathaniel.'

I clambered over the bulwark, aware that two men were rising to their feet from where they had been reclining on the deck beneath the shade of a canvas awning. One of them now spoke.

'Look, Lofty! It be Captain Devarre, just like what Nancy said. Praise be to the Good Lord!'

Startled, I looked closely at the short, plump, dark-haired man before me, and then at the muscular giant beside him with the straggling fair beard. Both wore round woollen caps, sleeveless canvas jackets and loose fitting breeches. I could hardly believe my eyes.

43

'Zebediah Watkins and Lofty Morris!' I exclaimed, and eagerly shook them both by the hand. 'I can hardly believe it.'

'Nor could we, Captain, when Nancy told us you be back,' said Zebediah. 'I lay my oath, you be the best captain we ever did sail under.'

'Except for Captain Kincaid,' I corrected him, recalling his words to me nine months earlier.

'Yes – well – I suppose there weren't nobody like him, God rest his soul,' he said uncomfortably. 'But we be proper glad to see you, Captain, true as true.'

'Zebediah has the right of it, none denying,' said Lofty. 'We be ready to follow you wherever you be wanting to go, Captain. You may lay to it.'

Nancy was now at my side.

'I hired these two old hands of yours last night tae guard the ship,' she said, clearly pleased with herself. 'And I can muster a suitable crew as soon as you like. I ken the ones that are seeking a ship tae replenish their funds for drinking and whooring.'

'Fine,' I said, and glanced around at the four-pounder cannons placed at intervals along the bulwarks, three on each side, and at the yawl, complete with oars, stowed forward near the bow.

I stooped beneath the long boom of the lowered gaff mainsail and descended the steps from the main hatch into the gloom of the hold, lit only by a single lantern. Forward stood a large stew pot upon an iron hearth with a red brick surround – the nearest to a galley that a vessel of this size could provide. The structure of the floor and side planking, reinforced by the upright timber futtocks, seemed quite sound. Stooped forward, I made my way aft. The one and only cabin in the stern was furnished with a small table, two chairs, a locker and a hammock slung from hooks in the low plank ceiling.

Everything was much as I had hoped for. Ascending the steps of the stern hatch to the deck, I briefly inspected the tiller and the wooden binnacle which housed the compass, then returned forward to the mast where my companions awaited me.

'All seems in order, Nancy,' I said. 'I'll be happy taking this craft to sea.'

'Where will we be bound, Captain?' asked Zebediah.

'Probably to Tortuga first, and from there to seize a rich prize,' I managed to answer confidently, even though I hadn't the faintest idea how I would amass my desired fortune.

'We be at your orders, Captain,' declared Lofty.

I thanked them both and followed Nancy down the ladder onto the wharf. I was content. I now had a good ship and two old hands I knew I could rely on. But there was something else in my mind – something I was unable to explain. I felt a sudden compulsion to take a stroll along the waterfront.

'Nancy,' I said, as we reached her carriage. 'Do you mind if I don't ride back with you? After being cooped up in a ship for nine weeks, I feel I need to stretch my legs for a while.'

'All right,' Nancy replied. 'But beware of suspicious characters.'

'They're all suspicious characters,' I pointed out.

'Ay, that's right. Dinny trust anybody.'

She smiled and climbed up into the carriage. Her Negro boy closed the door behind her before taking his seat beside the driver, who usually worked in the tavern cookhouse. I watched them drive off as I set out northwards along Fisher's Row. A few unsavoury looking individuals, in seafaring garb, strolled by or roistered on the timber verandas of taverns I passed, but I did not feel unduly concerned. When I had been in Port Royal before, I had learned to maintain a bold expression, confident in the knowledge that I had been a buccaneer myself – that I was, indeed, one of the Brethren of the Coast. It was a good feeling.

Now I was back on the account, as they called the trade of piracy. I had another ship, and a good one at that. Captain Kincaid had told me that a sloop was the buccaneers' preferred vessel, owing to its speed, agility and shallow draft. It could overtake or outrun larger, square-rigged ships, could sail more easily in a windward direction, and was more seaworthy in bad weather. Buccaneers relied more on their marksmanship with their muskets than they did on broadsides of cannon fire, since their principal intention was to capture and plunder Spanish ships – not destroy or sink them. But Kincaid had been one of the few who valued the prestige and heavy armament of frigates. These were, of course, the vessels I had had most experience of in the King's Navy, but for piratical escapades I was now inclined towards the majority opinion and rather looked forward to sailing the *Lady Corinne*.

Ahead of me to my left I could see the high wooden fencing in the sea, close to the shore. This enclosed several long, wide pens, known as turtle crawls. In the month of June, turtles were easily captured when they crawled ashore on the cays and beaches to lay their eggs. The aquatic reptiles were then stored alive within the pens in a foot or so of water until required for sale or consumption.

As I drew closer to these turtle crawls, I became aware of an angry voice uttering a stream of threats and curses, and two running figures came suddenly into my view, turning the corner of a timber shed at the top of the beach. The leading man wore only a cotton shirt and a cloth around his waist and loins. His bronze flesh and straight black hair told me instantly that he was an Indian.

His pursuer, a bearded, powerfully built seaman, now caught up with him and threw him to the ground. At this sight I recalled vividly being knocked sprawling on my back by just such a ruffian in that alleyway off Lime Street, after my arrival in Port Royal a year before. I could feel the shock and choking I had then endured and was now seized with uncharacteristic fury.

Just as the seaman drew a long-bladed knife from the sash around his waist, I yelled, 'Stop that, fellow! Leave that man alone!'

The seaman looked up angrily as I hastened towards him.

'This heathen son of a whore was trying to steal my turtle boat,' he exclaimed in a rage. 'I'm going to slit his gullet, skewer his guts and slice up his liver – the thieving dogfish!'

I swiftly drew my rapier and jabbed the point against his throat.

'And my blade will let out your evil soul if you as much as make him bleed,' I declared.

The fisherman's dark eyes blazed as he spoke.

'And who be you that you takes the side of a god-forsaken savage against a hearty sea dog?'

'Call him what you like, he's a human being. He may have wronged you, but he surely doesn't deserve to die.'

'A pox on you! Put down your sword and fight me fair.'

'But it wouldn't be fair. You're twice as strong as I am. Now begone, before I run you through.'

His eyes blazed again as he clearly considered tackling me, but when I pressed my rapier point firmly to his throat, he turned his head and spat on the ground.

'Then go to the Devil, you milk-veined coward!' he cursed. 'And take that sack of entrails with you.'

With that, he backed away and moved off down the beach, uttering obscenities. The Indian now rose as far as his knees and taking my left hand pressed his forehead to it.

'Good sir,' he said. 'You have saved my life. I shall be eternally grateful. May your god reward you.'

'Come on! Rise up,' I said, grasping his arm.

I helped him to his feet. He had a slim, lithe body and, I supposed, was not more than twenty years old. Looking into his dark brown eyes, I could see the genuine gratitude reflected therein.

'What is your name?' I enquired.

'I am called Cuesco.'

'Are you a slave?'

'Yes, sir. I am the slave of a merchant in New Street. This morning I was sent to buy lobsters and manatee from the fish market in High Street, as I often do.'

He indicated a bulging hemp sack lying nearby where he had dropped it on falling.

'So why did you try to steal the man's boat?'

'I wanted to go home, sir.'

'Home? Home to where?'

'To my village in what the Spanish call the Provincia de Tabasco.'

'Tabasco? Oh yes, on the Gulf of Mexico. I've seen it on charts. Are you a Mayan?'

'No, sir. I am not of the Maya. I am of the Ahualulcos people. We are of Aztec descent. My father is the *cacique* of my village – what you call chief.'

'How did you become a slave here in Port Royal?'

'I was seized by English seamen a year ago while hunting near the mouth of the river called Tonala. They brought me back to Port Royal and sold me in the market.'

'I see,' I said, feeling considerable sympathy towards him. 'You've had great misfortune.'

'Sir,' he pleaded. 'I beg you not to tell my master I tried to escape. He would be sure to give me a beating.'

'Have no fear, Cuesco. I won't say a word.'

'In truth, sir, I would rather not go back there. Can you help me to get away?'

I considered for a moment. Perhaps I could take him to Tortuga as part of my crew.

'Come with me,' I said. 'I'll hide you until I decide what to do with you. And bring your sack.'

I now began to walk back down Fisher's Row with Cuesco at my side, bearing his sack of seafood over his shoulder.

'Tell me,' I said. 'How did you hope to find your way back to your homeland in a turtle boat?'

'I hoped if I sailed in the direction of the setting sun I would eventually find it,' he replied.

'Far more likely you would have been carried adrift and died of thirst or drowned. But I admire your resolve in attempting such a foolhardy venture.'

'Sir, where will you hide me?'

'On my ship.'

'Your ship? You have a ship?'

'Yes, I'm a – I'm a Captain of buccaneers,' I stated with considerable relish.

'Oh sir, could you not take me to my home in your ship?'

'No, I'm afraid not. I'm after Spanish gold, and I have no time to spare for ferrying passengers.'

'But sir, if you took me back to my village, my father would reward you with all the gold you require.'

'Is that so?' I said sceptically. 'And where would your father get so much gold?'

'It is our gold, sir – Aztec gold that once belonged to the noble lord and emperor, Moctezuma. He had a treasure house full of gold sculptures, but when the Spanish came, they melted them all down into bars.'

I halted and looked closely into his eyes. He returned

49

my gaze firmly, showing no signs of mendacity, but I found his claim hard to believe.

'How did your people obtain it?' I asked cautiously.

'Sir, do you know about when, all those many years ago, the Spanish warrior lord, Cortés, and his men tried to leave the city of Tenochtitlan in the dead of night, bearing as much gold and treasure as they could carry?'

'Yes. I have read the account by the Spanish soldier, Bernal Diaz. When Cortés and his followers were preparing to cross the second canal on their portable bridge, they were attacked by the Aztecs from a multitude of canoes.'

'That is correct, sir. There was a great slaughter. Cortés escaped with some of his men, but they had to flee without their plunder. The gold was then taken back into Tenochtitlan, but not all of it. The ancestors of my father's family were fearful for their future, now that Moctezuma was dead, and dreaded that the Spanish might return with a bigger army and slay all the inhabitants of the city in revenge for their great losses. So, in the darkness and confusion, our ancestors slipped away in their canoes, taking twelve small chests of gold bars with them. During the months which followed, they trekked overland towards the rising sun until they settled in the land where we now live.'

I was beginning to believe his story. And why, I asked myself, would my guardian angel have prompted me to take a stroll up Fisher's Row, instead of returning with Nancy in her carriage, if the information I had thus received was false? Yet still I doubted.

'Even if your father is grateful to have his son returned to him, why would he agree to hand over to me gold that has been in the hands of his people for nearly a hundred and fifty years?'

'Sir, you have to understand that we do not value gold in the way that white men do. What use is gold to us

50

living our simple life in the forest? Apart from providing bright and shining ornaments, gold is a useless substance. It is no good for making axes, spears or tools. Our ancestors used the contents of four of the chests to create an idol of our chief god, Huitzlipochtli, and to make bracelets, pendants, rings and chains which have been passed down from generation to generation. The remaining eight chests were stored in a cave on a hillside where neither the Spanish, nor any other unwelcome persons, could find them, and they have lain there ever since, completely useless to us.'

I nodded and resumed walking.

'Believe me, sir,' said Cuesco, trotting alongside. 'My father will be overjoyed to have me back home. When he hears how you saved my life he will feel bound to honour my word and give you the reward I am promising you. After all, we have nothing else with which he could repay you. It is our strict rule, sir, always to pay our debts.'

'Very well, Cuesco, but you must understand that if I take you back to Tabasco and then find your story to be false, you will pay for your deception with your life. Angry buccaneers are not nice people.'

'I can believe that, sir. But I have no cause to worry, because every word I have spoken is true.'

I was convinced – almost.

'My sloop is down here,' I said. 'There are two good men on board who will treat you well and will be glad to have that sack of fresh food you are carrying. But you must not say anything to them or anyone else about the gold or where we are going until after we have sailed. I shall simply tell them that you are an escaped slave whom I have taken on as a member of my crew. Do you understand?'

'Of course, sir,' the Indian answered. 'I will say nothing.'

As we approached the wharf where the *Lady Corinne*

was moored, I was growing more and more jubilantly confident. It seemed that the quest I had set myself was not as idiotic as Nancy had supposed.

7

I found Nancy in her room, seated upon a stool at her tall desk, making an entry in one of her ledgers. It was impossible that she should have learned to read and write during her poverty-stricken childhood in the Grassmarket slums of Edinburgh, nor during her adolescent years selling her body on the streets, so I could only assume she had availed herself of tutoring once she had become prosperous in Port Royal. As Jonathon Kincaid had once said to me, Nancy was a survivor, and a very determined one.

She looked up as I entered, and laid down her quill.

'So you're back,' she said. 'There's a pitcher of kill-devil on the table there. Help yourself and pour one for me.'

I filled two tankards from the earthen pitcher before sitting down. Nancy rose, tossed back her mass of auburn curls and stretched herself with a slow motion, her magnificent breasts bulging above the lace border of her bodice. Once more, it was easy to forget about Corinne as my eyes devoured that voluptuous vision.

She came over, sat opposite me and picked up her tankard.

'Here's tae us,' she said, and drank heartily.

I drank also, but with small sips at first, savouring the exotic flavours of rum, lime juice, sherry and muscovite sugar. As I lowered my tankard, I spoke excitedly.

'Nancy, I have marvellous news. A miracle has happened.'

'A miracle?'

'Yes, a genuine miracle. My guardian angel has guided me towards a fortune in gold.'

Nancy shook her head.

'Och, I dinny think an angel would come tae Port Royal – unless he was a fallen angel.'

I knew she was making fun of my religious conviction, but I continued undaunted.

'Something told me to take that walk up Fisher's Row. It could only have been a divine intervention, because when I came to the turtle crawls I saved an Indian slave from being butchered by a fisherman.'

'You what?'

She began to take a serious interest now, as I related the whole sequence of events and what Cuesco had promised me. When I had finished, however, she remained unconvinced.

'Och, it all seems tae good tae be true, Nathaniel. He's probably just spinning you a yarn tae persuade you tae take him back home.'

'But when I told him my crew would kill him if his story proved false, he wasn't in the least shaken. Surely he wouldn't want to be taken home to Tabasco knowing he would then be killed. What would be the point?'

'Ay, I suppose that's true.'

Nancy took another mouthful of kill-devil and I did the same.

'Very well, Nathaniel,' she said with a sigh. 'I can see you're determined tae go ahead with this, and I'm reasonably persuaded by what you've been saying. I'll find you a crew from amongst my customers. A lot of the best men have already left for Tortuga, but I'll see who's available. How many do you want?'

'I thought about thirty.'

Nancy shook her head.

'You'd best think again. It doesny take that many men tae sail a sloop, does it?'

'No,' I answered. 'A fore-and-aft rig only requires a few

men. Indeed, I could probably sail her on my own if I had to. But it's best to have a body of musketeers along in case we run into the Spanish or even some hostile Indians.'

'Ay, but you've got tae consider what you're after. If you want tae go home with a fortune in gold, you dinny want tae have tae divide the spoils among thirty men. Let's face it – you dinny ken how big these eight chests are or how much gold is in them.'

'Cuesco described them as small chests, which they certainly must have been if the Spaniards had been hoping to escape, carrying them on their horses. Gold is pretty heavy stuff.'

'Exactly. So if you want tae be sure of getting a fortune, you have tae be prepared tae take risks. This could be your big chance, Nathaniel – maybe your only chance – but you have tae be bold if you want tae succeed.'

I looked into her eyes and banged the table with my tankard.

'You're right, Nancy. Fortune favours the brave, they say. I'll sail with a crew of … of ten, in addition to myself and Cuesco.'

'That's more like it,' Nancy declared, reaching over and squeezing my forearm. 'You already have Zebediah and Lofty. I'll find another seven before the day's out.'

'We'll need another eight,' I pointed out.

'No, we winny,' she replied. 'I'll be your eighth crew member.'

'You?' I exclaimed. 'I'm sorry, Nancy, but that's just not possible. Buccaneers have it laid down in their articles that under no circumstances can a woman be allowed aboard their ships.'

'Och, I ken about all that. But the men winny have any objection tae me. True, they look at my tits and maybe lust after me, but the buccaneers dinny regard me like they do other women. They ken how I deal with troublemakers in the tavern. Most of the boys take care no tae provoke me, and the few that dinny, live tae regret it. Believe me, Nathaniel, there winny be any problem.'

'I suppose you could be right,' I said dubiously. 'But why d'you want to come anyway?'

'Because it sounds like an interesting venture. I wouldny want tae go on a pirate raid, sacking some Spanish town, but a wee trip into the forest tae visit an Indian village will make a nice holiday for me.'

'I think you'll find a wee trip into the forest isn't much of a holiday,' I warned her. 'But on your own head be it. So what am I going to sign you on as – a seaman or a musketeer?'

'I'll be the ship's cook. I want tae be sure of what I'm eating.'

'That will be most satisfactory.' I paused. 'Bear in mind not to tell any of the men about the gold or where we're going. Just say they'll be guaranteed a good haul.'

'Ay. It'll be best tae keep our business secret till we've left Port Royal if we dinny want any thieving bastards following us. Well, Nathaniel, I must get back tae my accounting.'

Nancy leaned forward as she rose from the table, and as I stood up also, my eyes once more surveyed the two undulating mounds of her bosom. I could stand it no longer. Driven by a sudden, wild excitement, I hastened around the table and stood close to her.

'Nancy,' I said, looking steadily into her impish green eyes. 'When I was here last year, you told me that a woman likes to be taken and that I should learn to approach a woman with fire and confidence. So I'm going to take you now with all the fire that's burning within me.'

My heart was beating fast and I breathed more heavily,

further aroused by the proximity of her body and the scent of her perfume.

'Oh you are?' Nancy responded calmly. 'And how do you propose tae do that, Nathaniel? Are you going tae rape me?'

'If that's what's required,' I replied determinedly.

'Well, that'll make a change. I haveny been raped for fifteen years. Go ahead.'

With mounting excitement, I resolutely grasped her shoulders. Nancy's arms instantly interposed between mine and she buffeted my chest, at the same time hooking a heel behind my ankle. To my shock and dismay, I toppled backwards onto the wooden floor with a thud. Hitching up her gown and petticoat, Nancy leapt down upon me and straddled my stomach, then held my upper arms firmly against the planking. Desperately I strove to pull myself free from her grasp but was unable to do so.

Nancy smiled down at me.

'Do I take it you're no going tae rape me after all?'

'You take it correctly,' I muttered.

She rose and helped me to my feet, laughing heartily.

'Never mind, Nathaniel,' she said. 'Would you like me tae send one of my girls tae your room? You can have English, French, or African – whichever you would prefer tae relieve the pressure?'

'No thank you,' I replied. 'The only girl around here who could relieve my pressure is Scottish.'

Nancy frowned. 'Why are you so desperate tae stick your comparatively innocent prick up someone who has been fucked by a thousand men?'

'A thousand?' I queried, raising my eyebrows.

'Well, it might have been two thousand. I didny keep count. But I'd like an answer tae my question.'

'Very well, Nancy, I'll give you an answer. You may not have the luxuriant beauty of the women painted by Sir

Peter Lely or Pierre Mignard, but you have what I can only describe as a provocative voluptuousness and sexual allure that arouses my lust to an unbearable degree.'

She seemed momentarily stunned by my declaration.

'By my soul!' she exclaimed then. 'You've really got it bad.'

'Now, can I ask *you* a question?' I countered. 'If you've lain with two thousand men, how can you reasonably object to it being two thousand and one?'

'That's easy tae answer. Once upon a time when I was a whoor, I wouldny have objected at all. I'd by far have preferred a nice wee man like you tae some of the loathsome creatures I had tae go with tae keep from starving. But now that I'm well off, I only give in tae men I fancy, and – much as I like you, Nathaniel – I just dinny fancy you. It's as simple as that.'

'I understand,' I said, feeling humiliated once again. 'I'll leave you to get on with your work.'

As I walked to the door, Nancy called after me, 'I'll have those seven men ready tae sign up with you by this evening.'

'Good' was all I managed to say.

8

Nancy was true to her word. At six o'clock that evening, she ushered her seven men, accompanied by Lofty Morris, into my room. They responded reservedly to my initial words of greeting, eyeing me dubiously.

I drew Lofty to my side and asked him, 'How are you getting on with Cuesco?'

'He be no trouble, Captain,' Lofty replied. 'But Zebediah thought it best not to leave him alone on the ship.'

'Yes, that was best,' I agreed. 'Nancy said she'd find me a good crew. What d'you think of them?'

'Some of them be all right,' Lofty said in a noncommittal manner which I did not find encouraging.

I took a deep breath, feeling a trifle apprehensive, and addressed the seven buccaneers standing before me.

'You men don't know me,' I announced, adopting what I hoped was an authoritative tone. 'I am Captain Nathaniel Devarre. I was once a Master in the King's Navy and after that a Captain of buccaneers. Now, the venture upon which I am about to lead you...'

I was interrupted here by a gaunt and solemn looking individual.

'Begging your pardon,' he said in a strong Welsh accent. 'But if you are a buccaneer as you say you are, you must surely be mindful that you cannot yet call yourself our captain. For, look you, we have not chosen you as such in council, as is laid down in the laws of the Brotherhood of the Coast.'

'In the Devil's name!' Lofty exclaimed angrily. 'You

always were a lubberly sea-lawyer, Thomas.'

'What mean you by that?' the Welshman responded. 'You know very well, Lofty, that I only speak what is gospel true. We know nothing of this gentleman, and by my deathless soul, he does not look like a buccaneer captain to me.'

A clamouring chorus of 'aye' and 'true as true' arose from the men around him.

'Enough!' I called out. With feigned assurance, I then looked Thomas firmly in the eye. 'If you are calling me a liar, Thomas, we will have it out this very night with cutlass or pistol – whichever you care to choose!'

There was now a complete hush in the room as all eyes focussed on Thomas. I maintained a steady gaze, though secretly dreading he might accept my challenge.

'Look you, my friend,' he replied. 'I beg your pardon if my tongue has offended. I only mean to speak in reason. Our laws should be respected.'

I knew he was right, and although it was essential that I be in command of this venture, I really had no choice.

'Very well,' I said. 'We'll have a vote.'

Immediately, Lofty stepped forward and announced, 'Let me first tell you all that Zebediah and me sailed under Captain Devarre last year in a raid on Riohacha. He were the best captain we ever knew, excepting Captain Kincaid. Led us through fire and storm, he did, like a dare-and-be-damned hell-hound. May I sink and perish in blood if this be not true.'

I hardly recognised myself from this description, but I must say I was delighted by it. All this while, Nancy had been following the proceedings with a look of increasing irritation on her face. Now she broke her silence.

'You all kenned Captain Kincaid and what a great buccaneer he was. Would he have given one of his ships tae Captain Devarre if he didny ken he was of the right mettle? Of course he wouldny! And I'll lay to it that he's the only one among you knuckle brains who can navigate. There canny be any doubt about who should be captain here.'

Lofty now drew himself up, towering head and shoulders above us all.

'I propose Captain Devarre for captain,' he bellowed. 'Does anyone here say nay?'

He smacked his right fist into his left palm and cast his menacing eyes around the group of men before him. Nobody spoke a word.

'All in favour say "aye",' said Lofty.

'Aye,' one man responded without hesitation and the rest quickly echoed him, including Thomas, if rather sourly.

With great relief I now took command of the situation.

'Thank you, men. As your elected captain, I propose to have Zebediah Watkins as quartermaster and Lofty here as boatswain. All in favour say "aye".'

'Aye,' said the same man as before, followed by the others. The man who had spoken first on both votes now stepped forward. He was of medium build with a round, ruddy face and roguish eyes.

'May fair winds attend you, Captain Devarre,' he said in a lilting Irish accent. 'Rory McMullen's me name and, in faith, it was in me mind from the start, so it was, that you'd make a choice and lusty captain – God smite me blind and dumb if it wasn't. But might I ask the Captain whether the rest of the crew be drunk or hiding?'

'There aren't any others, McMullen,' I replied. As they looked from one to another in surprise, I continued, 'You all know privateering operations have been suspended by order of the Governor. As we don't want to sail out of Port Royal looking as if we are intent on making war, there'll just be this small crew. We'll sail under English colours, but we won't be flying the blood-red flag of the

61

buccaneers, and we won't be bringing any drums or trumpets.'

'To be sure, that's just as well,' said McMullen, 'because nobody here can play them.'

This brought a roar of laughter from the others and I went on with growing confidence.

'It is vital that our mission remains unknown in Port Royal, so I won't be telling you where we're going or why until we are out to sea. All I can say is that we'll be returning with more wealth than you've ever seen before and we won't have to fight any battles to get it.'

'Sure now, it's relieved I am to hear that, if this is all the men we're going to have,' said McMullen.

A bearded man asked, 'Begging your pardon, Captain, but how can we get plunder without fighting? It don't make sense – curse me for a papist, it don't!'

Others were muttering to one another, clearly distrustful of what I had told them. The Welshman, Thomas, now spoke up.

'Look you, Captain, I hope you haven't been foolish enough to believe some yarn about buried treasure.'

'No, I have not!' I declared irately, as the murmuring continued. I had to do something drastic to gain their confidence. 'I promise you I have a plan that will make you all rich men, and I further guarantee that if I do not keep this promise you have my permission to hang me from the yard-arm.'

McMullen responded, 'Oh, you may be sure we'll do just that, Captain. I give you me bible oath.'

A chill ran up my spine. How could I be sure that Cuesco's story wasn't a pack of lies? But I took some comfort in the fact that my pledge seemed to have reassured them as all murmurings had ceased.

'Now, in case you don't already know, Nancy will be joining the crew as ship's cook. I hope you can all accept

62

this and put aside any superstitious notions about women bringing bad luck to ships.'

Thomas said sharply, 'Look you, Captain, it is plainly laid down in our laws that no woman shall be brought aboard as a member of the crew. To do so is punishable by death.'

To my great relief, McMullen came to my aid.

'Oh, stow your blarney, Taffy. Faith, we wouldn't be wanting a woman aboard, sure we wouldn't. But we don't mind Nancy.'

The bearded man called out, 'Nancy be not a woman – she be a man with tits.'

They all cackled heartily at first, but fell silent as Nancy pushed two men aside and punched the speaker in the mouth, sending him tottering backwards.

'You be respectful of me, Billy Penryn,' she cried. 'Or by the Devil's twisted tail, I'll carve your gizzard and fry it for supper!'

With blood from his lower lip dribbling onto his black beard, Penryn glowered at her in silence. But McMullen was apparently unconcerned at the risk of incurring Nancy's wrath.

'Sure now, Captain,' he said. 'I'm thinking you'd best be telling Nancy that she'd better not be punching shipmates once we're at sea, if she doesn't want to be stripped to the waist and given thirty-nine lashes.'

The men roared with laughter once more and I couldn't help smiling myself.

Nancy glared at McMullen but before she could do anything, Lofty shouted, 'Have done with all this bilge and blather! Let's have a vote.'

I said, 'All in favour of Nancy aboard say "aye".'

All responded, except for Thomas and Penryn.

'Welcome aboard, Nancy,' I said.

'Only for this one venture,' she replied. 'Then I have

tae get back tae my life's work, which is tae see tae it that buccaneers can hae a few drinks and a few fucks before they die.'

This announcement brought laughter and cheers all round.

I held up my hand for silence. 'Then everything's settled. On the table over there you'll find a parchment upon which I have listed the articles under which we'll be sailing – exactly the same compensations, rules of conduct and punishments as you will have found on other buccaneer ships. I'll be claiming three shares of the takings as captain, and Zebediah and Lofty will each draw two shares. But I promise that the one share the rest of you will get will be far more than you've ever been paid before. Now sign, or make your mark.'

Thomas was the first to reach the table. He read the articles aloud in a clear voice and, to my relief, signed without complaint, as did everyone else.

'You will report here by noon tomorrow. We'll load up the sloop with provisions and sail the following morning. Here's hoping for a safe and profitable voyage.'

'Sure, we'll be drinking to that downstairs, so we will,' declared McMullen. 'Will you be joining us, Captain?'

'Of course,' I replied. 'I'm a buccaneer, aren't I?'

I expect my readers would like me to relate what transpired that night in the tavern, but in all honesty I remember little. Lofty had to leave in order to return to his duty guarding the ship, taking a bottle of rum to share with Zebediah. The rest of us sat around a table in the smoke-filled taproom. Pitchers of kill-devil kept coming and the yarns about Henry Morgan's audacious attacks on Portobello and Maracaibo, and what they all got up to with the Spanish women, grew less and less coherent.

McMullen pushed a buxom wench onto her back across

the table and had pulled up her frilled petticoat, before Nancy stormed over and ordered him to take her to one of the back rooms. Someone spilled a tankard of kill-devil onto someone else's lap and blows were briefly exchanged. Amid raucous cheers, I clambered unsteadily onto the table to dance a jig with an African harlot known as Jumping Joyce. The skirts of her bright red linen smock and white petticoat were tied up around her broad hips as she danced barefoot, a straw hat perched on the back of her closely curled hair and a red clay pipe between her lips. These details I do remember, but I had more to drink after that, and now retain only three brief images from later on: the flickering light of a single candle in a bracket above my bed ... the dusky eyes set widely in the pleasantly sculpted face which looked up at me ... the pert nipples standing out from her ebony flesh ... I am sorry. Try as I might, I can remember no more.

9

As dawn broke on the morning of Thursday, 1 July 1669, we cast off from our moorings, hoisted sail, and navigated the *Lady Corinne* across the cove and through the channel into the Caribbean Sea.

Fortunately, my quartermaster, Zebediah, had some experience of sailing a sloop of this design, and I had learned the art of making the best use of the wind with a fore-and-aft rig during a temporary assignment aboard one of the King's yachts in 1664. Consequently, I quickly regained my previous proficiency in positioning and adjusting the sails – a large, rectangular mainsail with the upper and lower spars, known as the gaff and the boom, secured by hinges to the single mast, and two triangular headsails – the staysail and jib – suspended on rope stays running from the top of the mast to the bowsprit.

At noon, I stood with my back to the sun and made a calculation of latitude by measuring the angle of the sun to the horizon with my backstaff. This enabled me to reckon from my chart that we had travelled nine leagues on our south-west course, running at a moderate speed before the wind. I now gave orders to man the sheets and turned the tiller so that the rudder moved to starboard as we tacked round onto a new course of west-north-west. With the prevailing north-easterly wind now on our starboard beam, our sails filled and our speed increased. Even with the south-east to north-west current in our favour, we were nonetheless required to tack slightly to windward at intervals in order to counter the leeward drift.

With all sails now trimmed, I summoned the crew to assemble amidships. They were clad in sleeveless jackets and loose knee-length breeches. I was similarly dressed, except that I had retained my plumed hat. Nancy, also in seafaring attire, a bright red kerchief tied around her auburn curls, stood beside me at the tiller. Cuesco, by the larboard bulwark, looked solemn, as always.

I raised my voice.

'Now men, the time has come to tell you where we are going and why. Cuesco here is the son of an Indian chief, and in payment for returning him to his village in the Gulf of Mexico, he will give us eight small chests of gold bars which came into the possession of his ancestors a hundred and forty-nine years ago.'

As I spoke these words, I became acutely aware of how unlikely this bizarre proposition sounded, and it was clear from the expressions on the faces before me that I was not the only one who thought so. There was a moment of deathly hush, interrupted only by a stamping of hooves from one of the four mules tethered to the bulwark at the bow.

It was McMullen who spoke. 'Sure, Captain, the mule doesn't seem to like that joke, so tell us another one.'

'It's not a joke, McMullen,' I declared. 'This gold was brought from an Aztec city that once stood where Mexico City is today. But gold is next to worthless to these Indians, and Cuesco has assured me his father will be happy to hand it over to us as a reward for saving his son's life and bringing him safely home. Think of it, men! Eight chests of gold divided amongst such a small number. Each share will be worth a fortune!'

I could see that the men were beginning to get interested, their lust for gold gradually vanquishing their former doubts. As their eyes began to glow, I lost no time in fuelling their avarice.

'You'll be the envy of every buccaneer in Port Royal. You'll have all the drink and all the women you want for years and years, and you'll be able to gamble with big stakes to your heart's content.'

Loyal and respectful, Zebediah now spoke up.

'Well, Captain, I always knowed you'd see us right, bless your heart. But I tell you true, your words do fill us with joy.'

A clamour of agreement followed.

'Aye.'

'Zebediah has the right of it.'

'We be much obliged, Captain.'

But just as, with enormous relief, I supposed all to be happily persuaded, McMullen spoke his mind.

'Faith, Captain, it's most eloquent you are in spinning us a happy yarn of the riches that are going to be bestowed upon us without us having to shed a single drop of blood to get them – just like the fairy stories me dear old mother used to tell me when she tucked me up in bed.' He looked now towards Cuesco. 'But I'm thinking you'd be best to warn this copper-skinned heathen that if he leads us to the end of the rainbow and there's no crock of gold there, we'll be hanging him from a tree upside down, so we will, ripping his innards out of his belly and stuffing them into his lying mouth.'

Cuesco glowered resentfully at McMullen but remained silent. Others now lent their support to McMullen's menacing words.

'We'll gut him like the scurvy dogfish he be!'

'We'll slice off his ears and cleave his skull asunder!'

My heart sank at this sudden reversal of mood, but Nancy came to my aid.

'Hold your whisht, you lubberly jackasses! Captain Devarre has something none of you have. He's got brains and he kens how tae use them. And if he says there'll be gold for all, then that's what there'll be. Pay no mind to that son of an Irish whore. I ken all about him. He ran off tae sea after he raped and murdered a tinker woman in Donegal and then put the blame on his friend, who was sent tae the gallows. Dinny pay any heed tae scum like him. You put your trust in Captain Devarre, and he'll lead you tae the gold.'

Lofty exclaimed, 'Nancy has the right of it. The Captain be a man of his word. I'd follow him to the bottom of the sea if that's where he said the gold was. May the Devil seize me if I lie.'

McMullen shook his head and spoke again, quite unperturbed.

'Sure, I think the Captain's a darlin' man, so I do. I'm only saying the boys should be prepared for possible treachery by the heathen. And Nancy shouldn't be telling these lies about me, charming girl that she is. I never laid a finger on that tinker bitch. It was me pal that done it, but I had to make a run for it because his brothers thought it was me. They wanted to carve me into little pieces, so they did.'

Thomas, the gaunt Welshman, now joined the discussion, having previously maintained his silence.

'Well, I say this. I don't trust McMullen because he always cheats at cards, but, look you, I have become convinced that Captain Devarre is an honest, God-fearing man who would not deliberately deceive us. He has promised to lead us to a fortune in gold and I am prepared to put my faith in his word. Let all those who pledge their faith in the Captain say "aye".'

'Aye!' now issued from every mouth except McMullen's.

'Sure, I'll say "aye" when I see the gold, so I will,' said the Irishman with a shrug.

I was, nonetheless, delighted with this outcome.

'Thank you, men. I swear I shall not let you down,' I

69

declared, with a confidence I did not feel. 'You can all return to your watch or your rest.'

To my surprise, Thomas spoke again.

'Look you, Captain, don't you think we should ask for the Good Lord's blessing on our voyage?'

'Of course, Thomas.'

I removed my hat and the others uncovered their heads also. Bowing my head, I offered up a short prayer.

'Almighty and everlasting God, by thy great mercy defend us from all perils and dangers at sea and on land, and grant us thy salvation and blessing; for the love of thy only Son, our saviour, Jesus Christ. Amen.'

'Amen,' came a chorus of voices.

'And deliver unto us the gold,' McMullen added, to my annoyance.

The men drifted away but Nancy remained at my side by the tiller.

'You must be more firm with them, Nathaniel,' she scolded. 'Captain Kincaid would never have put up with all that impertinent babbling from that dung-souled bilge-rat, McMullen.'

'They have the right to have their say in council, Nancy,' I explained. 'It's clearly laid down in their laws.'

'Och, I ken all that. But Jonathon didny allow their laws tae get in his way. He had the gumption tae assert himself as captain.'

With that, she departed down the rear hatch, leaving me resentful of her criticism. I had upheld the buccaneers' code of conduct and emerged triumphant in the end, hadn't I? We were now firmly on course to obtain a fortune for my Lady. I had every reason to feel satisfied.

I checked the compass and issued orders to the men on watch to man the sheets in order to tack a few degrees to windward. One advantage of a fore-and-aft rig is that all sheets and halyards can be handled from the deck

70

without anyone having to go aloft. The men were thus able to carry out my orders promptly and with greater ease than on a square-rigged vessel.

For the remainder of that day, and during the days that followed, the crew worked well without any dissension, even from McMullen, who turned out to be a proficient and normally good-humoured seaman. I had divided the men into alternating, four-hour larboard and starboard watches, under the charge of myself and Zebediah respectively. Cuesco was assigned to swabbing the deck and other menial tasks, all of which he performed without complaint. For her part, Nancy made good use of the iron hearth forward in the hold and provided us with a variety of meals from our provisions: barrels of salted beef, mutton, pork and sea turtle, augmented by potatoes, cabbages, peas, cassava bread, hardtack biscuits, cheese, bananas and plantains. We drank beer with our meals and kill-devil during off-duty periods, which were often spent playing cards or dice, though not for money, gambling being strictly forbidden aboard ships.

I permitted Nancy to sleep in the stern cabin, while I slung my hammock outside the cabin door. The remainder of the crew slept on deck. All lights had to be out by eight o'clock, at which time the commander of the watch toured the ship ensuring candles were extinguished, fire being a wooden vessel's greatest hazard.

I strongly suspect that some readers may be anxious to know what Nancy did in response to the call of nature, being on such a small ship with eleven men. She did exactly the same as the rest of us. She clambered out along the bowsprit, pulled down her breeches and projected her posterior over the sea below. Being wary of incurring Nancy's wrath, the men seemed always to look the other way while she was doing so.

In truth, the men preferred it when Nancy was not

around. They were unable to accept her as a member of the crew, even though she could be as crude in speech as any of them. Nonetheless, she appeared to be on good terms with everyone, even McMullen, despite her earlier condemnation of the Irishman.

Our second afternoon at sea found me manning the tiller, as I usually did for most of my watch. My clothing had been drenched during an earlier deluge of rain but was now drying nicely under the rays of the hot sun. The crew were mostly seated on the deck by the mast, chatting and joking with one another. Their current mood of relaxed and carefree camaraderie contrasted markedly with the previous afternoon's truculence.

Once more I began to wonder whether Cuesco's story about Moctezuma's gold was a fabrication to obtain his passage home. Did he perhaps have some plan to make his escape once we reached Tabasco? When that time came, I would have him carefully watched, I decided. Yet such doubts were fleeting. I remained hopeful that my guardian angel would guarantee Cuesco's sincerity and deliver his promise.

My only persistent concern was that Corinne might marry some wealthy aristocrat before I was able to get back to London with my fortune – the 'pots of money' which she had assured me would make her marry me without hesitation. But Corinne had been convinced that finding a wealthy suitor would not be an easy task. And surely my guardian angel would not have launched me on my present course of action if it was all to be for nothing? No. My beautiful Corinne was destined to be mine. I remembered her delightfully amiable disposition, her warm and inviting eyes, her delicious ivory flesh and her...

I had to stop. As always, such thoughts drove me crazy with desire for her. Oh, Corinne, I pleaded in my mind, please wait for me.

Dismissing this reverie, I glanced at the compass and adjusted the tiller slightly. The boom above my head creaked as the mainsail was pressured by the beam wind. Then I called Cuesco to me.

Wearing his habitual cotton shirt and loincloth, he came over to the tiller.

'Is there something that you want, sir?'

'Yes, Cuesco,' I replied. 'I want to know more about your people, the Ahualulcos. You told me they are of Aztec descent, but I assume they don't maintain the religious practices of Moctezuma's days.'

'Not wholly, sir. Since that time, our people have been subdued and reduced by the Spanish conquest and there has been much – what is the word you use? – absorption. That is a good word, is it not, sir?'

'Yes, Cuesco. Absorption is a very good word.'

'So there has been much absorption of culture and practices of the Maya and local customs in the region where my people have settled.'

'But there can't be many of the Ahualulcos still living free in the forest, as you say you do?'

'Oh no, sir. There are four Ahualulcos peoples – what you would call tribes – in the region of Chontalpa, that dwell in villages very much under the control of the Dominican priests who are converting them to Christianity – or, at least, they think they are converting them. Is converting the right word, sir?'

'Yes it is. And I suppose these peoples resent being ruled by the priests.'

'Of course. They present the Spanish with some difficulties, I believe, but most of the time they seem to accept their enslavement.'

'So why are your own people not enslaved?'

'We live in an area of the forest, surrounded by swamps, where the Spanish do not like to come. A few years ago, some priests and many soldiers came to our village and planted a cross in the ground and told us we should worship your Lord Jesus and his father and mother. When they went away, they carried off the gold idol of our god, Huitzlipochtli, and we took the cross down and hid it in our concealed cave on the hillside, where the gold is hidden, so that we could bring it out again if the Spanish should return. But, as I said, they do not care to come through the swamps and seem to have forgotten about us.'

'I see.' I glanced again at the compass. 'Are you able to feed yourselves well in the forest?'

'Of course, sir,' he replied. 'We hunt iguanas, parrots, turtles and manatees, and we have plantings of cassava, maize, beans, plaintains and papaya. We also grow cotton.'

'Very good,' I said, impressed. 'And your plantings always give satisfactory yields?'

'Yes, sir – provided we do not offend the gods by improper behaviour. Our people make regular sacrifices of animals to our gods in order to obtain the abundance of our plantings, that our women may give birth without too much pain, and that we will continue to receive water and sunlight.'

'Of course,' I said. 'The god of the sun was the principal deity of the Aztecs. Is that not so?'

'Yes, sir, and still is ours. We continue to worship Huitzlipochtli, but since the Spanish conquest, he no longer requires human sacrifice to allow the sun to arise every morning.'

'That's one good thing the Spanish did,' I said.

Cuesco looked at me sharply.

'Is that all you wish to ask me, sir?' he inquired.

'Yes, Cuesco. That's all for now.'

He nodded and returned to the larboard bulwark from which he continued to gaze out to sea.

Our voyage continued without incident, the crew seeming to maintain a harmonious camaraderie, until the morning of our fifth day at sea. I was once more manning the tiller, having earlier adjusted the sails to accommodate a variation of the prevailing wind to north-north-east, when I was approached by a rather worried-looking Zebediah.

'Begging your pardon, Captain,' he said respectfully. 'But there be some trouble. Thomas do wish us to hold a council over a disciplinary matter.'

I heaved a sigh.

'Oh, my God!' I said. 'What's happened now?'

'It be to do with McMullen,' he answered evasively. 'Thomas do know more about it than what I do.'

'Very well, Zebediah. Muster all hands amidships.'

'Aye, Captain.'

I sighed again. Only a few minutes before, I had been congratulating myself on how well everything was going. I should have realised it was all too good to last.

Once the men were assembled, and with Nancy standing on my right, Thomas spoke in his very precise Welsh voice.

'Look you, Captain, there is a matter of grave concern that requires our attention. McMullen has been visiting Nancy in her cabin at night while you are up here on watch.'

Shock, anger and bewilderment assailed me in equal measures.

'How do you know that?' I demanded.

'Because McMullen sleeps next to me, and the night before last he disappeared for a long time. So when he got up again last night, I followed him quietly down below in the darkness and I clearly heard the cabin door open and close.'

I turned towards Nancy who looked back at me sullenly.

'Is this true, Nancy?' I asked.

'What if it is?' she answered defiantly.

McMullen now spoke up cheerily.

'Faith, Captain, I've committed no crime. Our rules say that no woman should be brought aboard, so they do. So how can I have broken any law by obliging someone who shouldn't be here?'

Thomas said, 'Look you, Captain, McMullen speaks true – indeed he does – but his actions are nonetheless prejudicial to the common good insofar as they will arouse envy and resentment among the rest of the crew.'

'Aye!' exclaimed the bearded Cornishman, Penryn. 'If Nancy be making her cunt available to one, she should make it available to all. By the living thunder, she should! All or none, I says.'

Although I abhorred the very idea of this, I could not resist putting the proposition to Nancy.

'That sounds fair. What do you say, Nancy? Are you agreeable to making yourself available to all?'

'Go to the Devil!' Nancy retorted. 'I'm no whoor – no any more I'm not.'

'Then, might I suggest, Captain,' said Thomas, 'that we vote that fornication be prohibited aboard ship, on penalty of both guilty parties being subjected to Moses' law – forty lashes minus one upon the bare back.'

'Very well,' I said. 'All those in favour say "aye".'

'Aye!' was firmly returned by all, except McMullen and Nancy.

'So be it,' I said. 'The matter is closed. Crew dismissed.'

'Wait, Nancy,' I said quietly as they dispersed.

She turned to me, angry and resentful.

'I dinny want any lectures, Nathaniel.'

'I'm not going to give you a lecture,' I said. 'I just want to know why this happened.'

'Och, I was getting bored and I needed something tae liven things up.'

'And did McMullen liven things up?'

She smiled. 'Ay, he did that all right.'

I shook my head.

'But I don't understand. A few days ago you were calling him a dung-souled bilge-rat.'

'Och, I was speaking then in the heat of the moment.'

'But what about the tinker woman you said he raped and murdered?'

'Well, how do I ken if that's really true? Captain Lowther told me that story, but for all I ken, McMullen's version might be right. Maybe it *was* his friend that did it. Anyway, who am I tae judge? I haveny lived the life of a saint, have I?'

'No, I suppose not,' I agreed.

'What bothers you, Nathaniel, is that it wasny you I invited tae my cabin. You're jealous, aren't you?'

I looked into her mischievous eyes with a deep longing.

'You know I am,' I answered in a subdued voice.

She patted my arm.

'You shouldny admit these things so freely, Nathaniel. If you give a woman the impression that you're desperate for her, she's more likely tae mess you about.'

With that, she turned and headed for the stern hatch. My eyes lingered on the curves of her buttocks revealed by her tight breeches. The very thought that someone like McMullen could have her but not me was a source of frustration and dismay.

Late that afternoon, we sighted the east coast of Yucatán on the horizon ahead of us. I immediately altered our course to north by west. We consequently made slow progress, with the wind on our starboard bow and sails close-hauled, until the following day when I changed course to west by south, which put the wind indirectly behind us on our starboard quarter. Two days later, I once more altered course, this time to south-west as we headed into the Gulf of Mexico. Now, with the wind directly astern, and tacking to larboard periodically to counter the drift caused by the current, we sailed for nearly two more days before at last sighting the coast of Tabasco on our larboard bow just after five o'clock in the evening of Saturday, 10 July 1669.

As soon as I heard the lookout's cry of 'Land ho!', I issued orders to heave to and put the tiller hard over to larboard. My men promptly close-trimmed the mainsail and backed the jib, as the bow of the *Lady Corinne* headed into the wind. Shortly, the ship came to a halt, apart from a slight drift, and thus we remained, with reefed sails, until darkness had fallen, when we proceeded once more on our south-west course towards the gold that I could only pray was awaiting us.

10

As dawn broke the following morning, the coastline ahead of us gradually took shape. With Cuesco close by, at the larboard bulwark, I scanned the continuous vista of sand, rocks and palm trees until spotting what appeared to be the entrance to an inlet.

'We are close, sir,' Cuesco exclaimed excitedly. 'We are very close. That is what the Spanish call the Barra de Santa Ana. The Rio Tonala is only a short distance to the west of it.'

My guardian angel was surely with me. I sent up a silent prayer of thanks that my navigational skills had not let me down. After consulting my chart, I altered course to west-south-west and, as our sails filled from the wind on our starboard quarter, we maintained a fair speed through the gentle waves. For the next two hours, Cuesco grew more and more excited until he suddenly uttered a loud whoop.

'There, sir!' he cried. 'There is the mouth of my river. There is the Rio Tonala.'

I could clearly see the indicated break in the continuity of the palm-lined shore.

Joyously I called out, 'This is it, men! There is the river that will lead us to the gold!'

A loud cheer arose from all sides.

'Praise be to the Lord Jesus!' exclaimed Thomas.

'Indeed, Thomas, indeed,' I said, delighted.

We tacked to leeward and sailed into the mouth of the river with the wind now on our larboard quarter. On my orders, Lofty supervised the loading of our six cannons with gunpowder and round shot. Cuesco had assured me we were unlikely to meet any Spanish craft on this river, but I wasn't taking any chances.

The river mouth was fairly wide. Coconut palms with spreading green fronds, hibiscus trees with heart-shaped leaves and pale yellow flowers, and sea grape with clusters of fruit hanging amidst large, shiny leaves grew in profusion along both banks. We regularly measured the depth of the water with a knotted lead line, though the sloop's shallow draft ensured there were always several fathoms to spare.

After an hour had passed, the river narrowed a little. To larboard, the bank was resplendent with palms and cordia trees hung with orange-scarlet flowers, but to starboard lay what appeared to be an extensive area of mangrove swamp. Viewed from this distance, the swamp had a deceptive appearance owing to the lush beauty of its greenery. We had sailed past the seemingly endless mangrove trees for perhaps fifteen minutes when Cuesco suddenly looked round at me.

'Here, sir! We must stop here and proceed on foot through the swamp.'

I turned the tiller, heading the *Lady Corinne* towards the mangroves, while the men alternately trimmed and eased the sheets. Zebediah carefully tested the depth with his lead line and, once I had decided we were as close as we could safely go, I turned the ship parallel to the tree line and ordered hands to halyards to lower our sails, after which we dropped anchor.

All was now bustle on board as we prepared for the next stage of our great adventure. The four mules were fed and harnessed, then loaded with two water casks, four sacks of fodder and another sack containing chains and coils of rope. We packed no food supplies for ourselves

80

as Cuesco assured me we would reach the village in a few hours where he promised we would be well fed. To maintain our strength until then, we now ate a cold meal before setting off. The men were all in good spirits and there was considerable banter between them as they ate.

When I saw that Zebediah had finished, I summoned him aft where I had been studying my chart of the region. I took comfort in the feeling of reliability his chubby appearance always gave me. Throughout the voyage he had proved himself a most satisfactory choice of quartermaster.

'I'm afraid I'm going to have to leave you behind, Zebediah,' I told him. 'I need someone trusty to look after the ship.'

'Bless your heart, Captain, that be no matter,' he replied. 'It be certain I have no wish to go among them heathen savages.'

'I'll leave Barstow and Hershey with you. That's the most I can spare. Be sure and have someone on watch at all times. I hope no Spaniards will come this way, but if they do, they will surely make trouble. Even though we're supposed to have ended hostilities, the Spanish won't take kindly to an English vessel making an incursion into their waters.'

'Have no fear, Captain. You can lay to it that I'll keep the ship safe for you. There's the truth of it.'

'God willing, we'll be back tomorrow, by early afternoon. Keep a watch for us and be ready to lower the yawl when you see us coming.'

'Aye, Captain. I'll be doing that with a will.'

'Thank you, Zebediah. I have complete faith in you,' I said, wishing I could say the same about everyone in the crew.

The one other person in whom I had complete faith was my boatswain, Lofty; because of this and his giant stature, I was most grateful that he would be coming ashore with me. I now lost no time in mustering Lofty and the rest of the selected group – namely, Thomas, McMullen, Penryn, Ross and Wentworth. Lofty had already issued them all with cutlasses, muskets, pistols and ammunition. They stood before me now, seeming eager to be on their way. Their upper bodies were crisscrossed with leather baldricks, bandoliers and straps supporting cartridge boxes, powder horns and priming flasks. Like them, I had armed myself with a long-barrelled, heavy calibre, flintlock musket, in addition to two pistols thrust beneath my sash and a cutlass suspended from my leather baldrick.

Nancy now came up from below and joined the group. I would have preferred her to remain behind on the ship, but she insisted she was coming with us. She wore a shirt and loose breeches like the rest of us, but was unarmed.

'Don't you want a pistol?' I suggested.

'Och, what would I want with one of thon things?' she retorted scornfully.

'Very well,' I said with a shrug, and then addressed all of them. 'Now listen carefully, everyone. The yawl will take us as far as the mangrove trees in four trips, transporting one mule at a time. We'll then wade through the swamp in single file. I'll take the lead with Cuesco as guide. Nancy will be behind me, then McMullen. Thomas, Penryn, Ross and Wentworth will follow, each leading a mule. Lofty will be last man, keeping an eye on the rest of you and ready to help if one of the mules gets in trouble.'

Thomas said, 'Begging your pardon, Captain, but I respectfully suggest that it would be best for Nancy to remain behind on the ship. Swamps are very nasty places; indeed they are.'

Before I could reply, Nancy exclaimed, 'Stow your

blethering, you whining sea-lawyer! I've spent half my life in nasty places.'

'There's your answer, Thomas,' I said. 'Nancy will be coming with us. One more thing, lads. Watch out for snakes and crocodiles.'

'But look you, Captain,' persisted Thomas, clearly undaunted by Nancy's scolding. 'Am I not right in saying that the fearsome reptiles to be found in countries of the New World are alligators?'

'Alligators are much more common in the Americas, Thomas,' I replied. 'But there are crocodiles in a few regions, and this is one of them.'

McMullen said, 'Sure, Taffy, if one of those big fellows grabs you in his jaws, you won't care what he's called, sure you won't.'

This drew laughter from everyone except Thomas. The men were clearly in good spirits, which augured well.

McMullen spoke again.

'Captain, what's to be done if somewhere along the way, Cuesco takes it into his head to make a run for it, knowing he's been lying to us?'

'I am quite sure that won't happen, McMullen,' I replied impatiently.

'But faith, what if it does?'

I hesitated for a moment, then answered firmly, 'The man nearest to him will shoot him. Now, enough jawing, men. Let's lower the yawl and get that gold.'

11

Cuesco moved slightly ahead of me as we waded waist-deep through the murky, foul-smelling swamp. The stench of decay, the heat and the humidity were oppressive and my shirt was soaked by the perspiration that constantly streamed down my chest and back. The surrounding red mangrove trees had shiny, dark green leaves and small clusters of yellowish flowers upon their spreading branches. I struggled onwards around their formidable roots that arched upwards well above water level.

Now that he was back in his home territory, Cuesco had disposed of his shirt and wore only his loincloth. The sweat dripping beneath his long, black hair and running in rivulets down his bronze back showed me that exertion in this humid atmosphere was affecting him almost as much as the rest of us. I was careful to keep my musket primed and above the water level, ready for use should Cuesco suddenly decide to make his escape. Yet I remained convinced that such an eventuality would not occur. Cuesco could not be false, I reasoned, else why would my guardian angel have guided me to him in the first place?

We halted while the men behind me hacked away some intertwined foliage with their cutlasses to make easier passage for the mules. I glanced at Nancy who stood behind me, waist-deep in swamp water, sweat streaming down her decidedly weary face.

'Are you enjoying your wee trip into the forest, Nancy?' I enquired.

Ignoring my facetious question, she said, 'What can I dae about this? It winny pull off.'

She indicated the leech clamped onto the side of her throat.

'No,' I said. 'It's already dug in and sucking your blood. If you managed to pull it off and left the head inside, the wound would fester. Just leave it alone for now.'

After breaking off a twig from a branch above my head, I pointed to another leech on the sleeve of Nancy's shirt. The creature's narrow tip wavered as it felt its way forward. Then, as it arched its body to advance, I swiped at it with the twig, knocking it into the water.

'You have to get them when they release their grip to move,' I explained.

I dealt similarly with a leech crawling up the front of my own shirt.

The mules now struggled forward again and our laborious march resumed. In addition to leeches, we were also assailed by clouds of sand flies and the inevitable mosquitoes, whining around our ears and inflicting sharp bites on all parts of our upper bodies. Another problem was that our boots kept getting stuck in the thick mud of the swamp's bed. We had repeatedly to extricate them by twisting our feet from side to side. At half-hour intervals we rested briefly, so that we could have a drink of water from our casks and rid ourselves of leeches as best we could.

So we continued across that foul morass in a west-south-west direction, clambering between tree trunks and roots, pestered by insects, suffocating in the hot and fetid air and eventually close to exhaustion. Fortunately, we did not encounter any crocodiles. (These, I later learned, were usually deterred from entering mangrove swamps by the profusion of giant roots.) But at one point I had to warn Nancy to duck aside in order to avoid two slim, green vipers hanging precariously from foliage overhead.

After two hours of this ordeal, during which we undoubtedly did not cover as great a distance as our exertions warranted, the swamp grew shallower as we reached higher ground. Shortly, we found ourselves wading only knee-deep among black mangrove trees, the roots of which did not always emerge above the water and consequently had to be continually stepped over; nevertheless, the going was easier than it had previously been. The branches of these different trees sprouted narrow, pointed leaves and clusters of small white flowers.

In another half-hour or so, we emerged, with sighs of relief, from this waterlogged soil onto dry ground. We gratefully lay down upon the leaf-strewn ground to regain some of our strength before we slaked our thirst and attended to the leeches. We discovered these were liberally distributed about our bodies and it took us some time to remove them all from our flesh. I ignited a small pile of leaves and shoots with my tinderbox, and we then applied the smouldering tips of twigs to those drinking their fill of our blood. It was with considerable relish that we watched the creatures curl up and fall away.

When I had burned two leeches from Nancy's throat, she took the twig from my hand, blew upon it and disappeared behind a large cluster of ferns to rid herself of one feeding upon her bosom. A roar of laughter arose when the Cornishman, Penryn, observed, 'Look, boys! McMullen be such a sex-fiend, he's even got a leech pleasuring his prick!'

'Well sure, I can't be getting Nancy to do that for me any more, now can I?' McMullen retorted as he burned the creature from his appendage.

This brought further guffaws and McMullen looked across at me.

'Pardon me, Captain. It's hoping I am that I haven't offended you.'

He had offended me, without doubt. I was as jealous as hell of his intimacies with Nancy.

'Be careful, McMullen,' I said, restraining my anger. 'I am a tolerant person but I do have a limit.'

'Oh, it's sure I am that I wouldn't be wanting to cross your limit, Captain. By all that's holy, I wouldn't.'

I noted his smirk as he spoke. He wasn't afraid of me. People rarely are.

In the meanwhile, Lofty had placed one of the water casks upon the ground. He removed the lid and allowed the mules to drink from it, one after another.

Ross, a fair-haired Devon lad of only nineteen years, looked on with disapproval.

'Be we going to have to drink that water after them dirty animals have been slurping from it, Lofty?' he protested.

'Sweet merciful heaven!' Lofty exclaimed. 'You've just been wading for miles through mud what smells like shit, and you've been eaten alive by leeches and all manner of flies and bugs in this fever-ridden wilderness, and you be worried about drinking water after four well-deserving animals? Hellfire and brimstone! What kind of a baby be you, Ross?'

'Don't you be calling me a baby!' Ross retorted irately.

Lofty drew his giant frame up to its full height.

'Why?' he asked brusquely. 'What be you going to do about it, eh?'

'I be going to do nothing,' Ross sullenly replied.

'Verily, that be most wise, lad,' Lofty said in a kinder tone. 'Now you see what you can be doing to remove the leeches off the mules.'

Wentworth, a normally taciturn man in his early forties, mumbled, 'That be not fair. We've been nursing these beasts all morning.'

'Don't be giving me that bilge, Wentworth,' Lofty declared. 'You be giving Ross a hand, and look lively.'

Ross and Wentworth tackled their task without another word. I greatly envied Lofty. It seemed to me that men whom God had blessed with physical stature had an enormous advantage in this world – at least, in obtaining respect and imposing their will.

Nancy had now returned from behind the cluster of ferns and lay down upon the grass and leaves in silence. Thomas approached me cautiously and spoke in a low voice.

'Look you, Captain, I rather think Mistress Nancy is regretting that she did not heed my advice and stay on the ship, and no mistake.'

'You may be right, Thomas,' I said. 'I was wondering about that myself.'

'I tell you truly, Captain, I am very concerned for her; indeed I am. She may be foul-mouthed and an unrepentant fornicator, and I have seen her fight a drunken buccaneer in the tavern and lay him out cold – let me rot and perish if I lie – but look you, Captain, she's still a woman and it is not fitting for a woman to be wading through swamps and suffering the agonies and perils of this devil's garden; indeed it is not.'

'All that you say may be true, Thomas,' I conceded. 'But I don't advise you to say that to Nancy.'

In the past few minutes the sky had darkened and rain now began to fall, first in isolated drops, then rapidly increasing into torrents. Men resting on the ground quickly rose to their feet.

'All right!' I proclaimed loudly, competing with the roar of the storm. 'Let's be on our way!'

'Have we far to go, Cuesco?'

'It is not too far, sir,' he answered vaguely. 'Let us hope this is just normal afternoon rain. We are entering a period when it can rain continuously for eight or ten days.'

'Very well. Lead the way,' I said.

Feeling rather despondent, I glanced behind me at Nancy who looked bedraggled and miserable. I wondered again if she wished now she had remained on the ship.

Cuesco led us along a narrow trail through the forest, still maintaining a west-south-west direction, as I ascertained from my pocket compass. The ground beneath our feet was rapidly being transformed into mud by the deluge. Disordered vegetation bordered and encroached upon the trail. The trees were huge and thick vines hung from their branches. From some trunks spikes projected while others were deformed and bent towards the ground, amidst thickets of bushes and ferns and interwoven creeping plants.

However, I was conscious only of the clamminess of my drenched clothing upon my weary body, the constant stream of water spilling from the brim of my hat and the squelching of my boots in the mud. And all the while, continuous effort was required to duck beneath low branches and vines, brush aside palm leaves and ferns and clamber over fallen tree trunks. When we stopped to rest, we leaned against wet trees in miserable silence, the rain relentlessly beating down upon us, so that we were glad to move on as quickly as possible.

To our relief, the rain stopped after two hours and we continued through the dripping forest, growing ever more weary, yet warmed, and to some extent cheered, by the return of the sun, the squawking of parrots and the occasional chatter of monkeys amongst the overhead foliage. After another hour, Cuesco turned towards me, his eyes dancing with excitement.

'We are nearly there, sir,' he exclaimed. 'I will soon be home.'

12

The village lay in a clearing on higher ground beneath the shadow of a hill. We approached through the trees and shrubbery, crossed a shallow stream and continued up a gentle slope. I felt suddenly apprehensive. It had just occurred to me that we had been concerned all along that, if Cuesco was deceiving us about the gold, he would try to make a run for it once we had landed him in his native territory. But why would he take such a risk, with our muskets at his back, when all he had to do was lead us to his village where our small party could easily be overpowered? I remembered then the village of the Carib Indians near Riohacha the previous year and the Spanish woman and her son bound to stakes, waiting to be roasted alive.

I gestured to halt, and ordered my men to reprime their muskets and pistols, ignoring Cuesco's impatience at this delay. We were soon on our way, however, Cuesco growing so excited I had to restrain him from breaking into a run.

From the clearing immediately ahead of us came the sound of alarmed voices. As we glimpsed thatched roofs through the foliage, half-a-dozen Indians suddenly appeared on the trail before us, brandishing feathered wooden shafts with stone points. I heard hammers being cocked behind me.

'Don't fire, men!' I commanded. 'For God's sake, don't fire!'

Cuesco now ran towards the Indians, babbling excitedly in a strange tongue. The astonishment and joy upon their faces was unmistakable. They lowered their spears and crowded around Cuesco, embracing him, all chattering at once. One of them ran back into the clearing, yelling at the top of his voice.

'Come on, sir,' Cuesco called back to me. 'Welcome to my village. It is perfectly safe. Come on.'

We followed him and his fellow Indians into the clearing. On both sides of a level, rectangular area were numerous round wooden dwellings with roofs of thatched palm leaves and straw. The smoke of cooking fires escaped from openings in the thatchings. At the far end of the rectangle stood a large house on its own, from which emerged at least a dozen excited people to join all the other village inhabitants crowding onto the cleared area with overjoyed expressions and babbling ecstatically. All wore loincloths and headbands of brightly coloured cotton; they had long black hair and copper-coloured skin.

The group from the far dwelling attempted to embrace Cuesco all at once. There were joyous exclamations and the women were in tears. It was wonderful to behold. Then, silence fell as Cuesco explained to his family how this apparent miracle had occurred. The eyes of the other villagers remained fixed upon the family; for the moment, we were ignored.

McMullen commented, 'Sure, it's like one time back in Donegal when I'd been let out of gaol. Me dear old mother cried buckets, so she did.'

Cuesco summoned me. I took a deep breath and made my approach, very aware of all the curious eyes now upon me. I noted that the grey-haired man, standing beside Cuesco, wore a cotton belt and headband decorated with coloured stones. On his wrists were gold bracelets and a necklace of finely-worked gold hung from his neck.

'Sir, this is my father, the *cacique*,' Cuesco said as I reached them.

I thoughtlessly held out my hand to the chief and then quickly withdrew it as he grasped both of my upper arms and spoke three short sentences. He was, I estimated, at least sixty years old, with a strong but solemn countenance. He did not smile as he spoke but I could tell from the brightness of his eyes that he was undoubtedly pleased with me. Also bright were the exquisite tiny gold chains suspended from his ears and nostrils.

Cuesco translated the chief's words.

'My father rejoices and gives you his eternal gratitude for having saved my life and for having brought his much loved son safely home to him. He says you are all his welcome guests.'

The chief released his hold on my arms and spoke again. This time, the expression in his eyes, like the tone of his voice, was serious, even severe. Cuesco bowed his head and spoke in careful tones.

'My father says that the Lord Moctezuma's gold was sacred to our ancestors and is, therefore, something that cannot be easily given. But he feels bound by the good faith of the Ahualulcos peoples to honour my promise to you. He will be willing to make this great sacrifice because you have given back to him that which he holds most precious in this world.'

Greatly relieved by these words, I said, 'Please convey to your father my profound thanks for his generosity and most worthy pledge of honour.'

Cuesco began to translate but the chief indicated with a gesture that he should be silent. Then he spoke again.

Looking anxious, Cuesco said, 'Sir, my father says, however, that he must first consult with the elders of our people, but he is hopeful that his decision will be upheld.'

'I see.' I was decidedly worried by this new proviso. 'Tell him what I said before and add that I myself place great value on honouring debts and promises, and greatly respect others who do the same.'

Cuesco delivered my statement, whereupon the chief gave me a long, appraising look before speaking again.

'My father says you will not find him wanting in good faith,' said Cuesco, 'nor any of our people. He also says he will be pleased to provide you and your people with food and lodging for the night.'

As he spoke, the chief turned away and began yelling instructions to at least three different groups of his people who, I noticed, looked rather sullen as they dispersed.

Cuesco said, 'Will you bring your followers into our house, sir, and share our food?'

Fearing that one or more of my men might behave in some inappropriate manner which would give offence to the chief's family, I shook my head.

'No, Cuesco. Convey my thanks to your father for his kind invitation, but I feel that your family should be allowed to celebrate your return without the presence of strangers. We will rest in the shade of one of the houses. If it's not too much trouble, perhaps our food could be brought to us there.'

'Very well, sir,' Cuesco said, seeming to accept the reason I had given him. 'I am sure I can arrange that. And I want to say to you, sir, that in my eyes, not even the gold can sufficiently repay you for saving my life and bringing me home.'

'I can assure you, Cuesco, that once the gold is safely in my hands, I will be repaid to my full satisfaction.'

'That makes my heart glad, sir. I will have the eight chests brought to you from our hidden cave just as soon as the elders have approved my father's decision.'

I resisted the temptation to threaten him with dire consequences if the chests of gold were *not* handed over. Instead, I simply thanked him and returned to where my men were waiting in the centre of the clearing. With approval, I noted that Lofty and Wentworth were providing the mules with fodder and water.

A large number of the village inhabitants had gathered round our party, but not too closely. They appeared very curious about these fair-skinned strangers who had suddenly appeared in their midst, but displayed no signs of friendliness. Indeed, there was definite hostility in the faces of the younger men, while the women remained at the rear, though peering inquisitively over the shoulders of their menfolk. McMullen greeted me.

'Sure, Captain, I'm thinking these heathen savages would like to put us all in the pot for supper, so they would.'

'Well, you're wrong, McMullen,' I said. 'In fact, they're going to provide us with supper right away. Come on, men, let's seat ourselves down in the shade of that house.'

The Indians moved aside as I led the way to the dwelling I had indicated. The space between it and the next one was in the shade, and we settled down in a rough semi-circle, very glad to be off our feet after the exhausting march through the swamp and forest. The Indians seemed to have lost interest in us now and began dispersing to their houses. Ross, the youngest of our number, had clearly been disturbed by McMullen's words.

'Be these savages really cannibals, Captain?' he asked.

'No, they're not,' I replied. 'They may be primitive, but they're probably no more savage than we are. So stop worrying.'

'Faith, Captain,' said McMullen. 'If they're as savage as us buccaneers, I'd say we've got plenty to worry about, so we have.'

Some of the men laughed.

'What be happening about the gold, Captain?' Lofty asked.

'That's all arranged,' I said, endeavouring to sound more optimistic than I felt. 'They'll be bringing it to us shortly.'

A dozen Indian women now approached, bearing calabash bowls and earthen pots. Apart from short cotton skirts, they wore no other attire and, strangely, were generally plumper than the invariably spare males. Their naked breasts wobbled as they bent to lay the vessels on the ground before us.

'Devil burn me!' Penryn exclaimed. 'Look at the size of them tits!'

All eyes, including mine, were already fixed upon the dangling globes of tawny flesh.

'You can look, men, but for God's sake don't touch,' I warned. 'If you value the gold and your lives, it is vital we don't do anything to offend these people.'

'And I thought mine were big,' Nancy commented.

'Sure now, Nancy darlin', yours are magnificent, so they are,' said McMullen. 'And I should know,' adding with a smirk, 'sorry, Captain.'

The women's faces remained expressionless, but I noticed they kept looking at Nancy's auburn hair. They didn't utter a word the whole time and swiftly departed across the clearing.

Thomas observed, 'These people are not very sociable; indeed they are not.'

The bowls were filled with an assortment of cooked meats: iguanas, other lizards and birds, as well as sweet potato and papaya. It tasted well enough to hungry mouths like ours. Even so, Wentworth grumbled.

'God rot their heathen bones! This be the Devil's shit.'

But the miserable Wentworth was rarely pleased with anything. The pots contained fresh water, presumably from the nearby stream.

Penryn said, 'It be a pity we didn't bring no rum with us. You headed wrong there, Captain.'

95

'Oh no, I didn't,' I answered. 'The last thing I want is you lot getting drunk and running around the village, causing havoc with the women.'

'Never mind,' said Nancy. 'You'll soon be back in Port Royal, causing havoc with the girls at the Sea Horse. I canny wait tae get back. You can keep your sea rovering. If I'd kenned what it was going tae be like, I wouldny have come. I'd rather be a whoor again than live like this.'

'It's sure I am, Nancy, that the boys would be most pleasured by hearing how you sold your broth of a body on the streets of Edinburgh,' ventured McMullen. 'How much did you charge?'

To my surprise and dismay, Nancy was not reticent on this matter.

'For most of them that used tae have me against the wall up a close in the Grassmarket or the High Street, I used tae charge a shilling, but for gentlemen that had me on my back in their coaches, I'd charge two crowns. Mind you, if they'd had a few drinks, I could sometimes get more.'

'What if they refused to pay?' asked Penryn.

'I'd draw my dirk – you ken, my wee dagger – and I'd get my money; dinny you worry.'

Lofty brushed some particles of food from his straggling beard and expressed some doubt.

'But Nancy, there must have been some big fellows with more muscle than you, I'll warrant.'

'Och, aye. There was a few hulking brutes over the years that had their way with me and then left me bruised and bleeding, and maybe helped themselves tae my night's takings. But there wereny many who found they could get the better of me, I can tell you.'

Although Nancy had previously told me some details of her life of poverty and degradation in Edinburgh, I was still amazed by what I heard. I greatly admired her courage and will to survive and the fact that she had eventually won through to become a comparatively wealthy tavern keeper.

As we were consuming the last of the food and water, Cuesco appeared from beyond the adjacent wooden house. He faced me with bright eyes and smiling lips, his voice excited as he recited his latest news.

'Sir, I am most pleased to tell you that although the elders declared I was wrong to promise you the gold, my father was able to persuade them it was necessary to pay our debt for my life and safe return. Otherwise, our lack of good faith would surely bring punishing disasters to our crops and our lives. Sir, the gold has now been brought down from the cave on the hill and awaits your approval.'

'Splendid!' I exclaimed and leapt to my feet. 'Show us the way, Cuesco.'

Bringing our four mules with us, we followed the Indian towards the top of the cleared area. Many villagers – men, women and children – started to emerge from their round dwellings. We shortly reached one such building with a small door that required me to bend forward as I followed Cuesco inside in a state of mounting excitement. The interior was spacious, clean and well constructed, with small windows that would admit little rain but gave sufficient light. A clay griddle stood in the centre of the earthen flooring. Expertly woven cotton hammocks – exactly eight, I counted later – were suspended between upright poles driven firmly into the floor. I marvelled at the speed and expertise with which this had been prepared, but I could see no chests.

'Where's the gold?' I demanded anxiously.

'Right behind you, sir,' Cuesco replied.

I turned and, to my relief, saw eight small chests standing

against the wall near the doorway. The others of my party had by now stepped inside and eagerly gathered round.

'Well, there they are, lads,' I exclaimed triumphantly. 'Here's what we came for.'

The hardwood money-chests were of typical early sixteenth-century manufacture, and, thankfully, not padlocked. A hush descended as I bent over one of the chests and, with trembling hands, I loosened the hinged metal flap from the ring and raised the lid.

There they were! Bright, shining gold bars greeted my eyes – the produce of the melted down artefacts of the Emperor Moctezuma's treasure. My hazardous and unlikely quest for a fortune had not been in vain.

As I hurriedly opened the remaining seven chests to confirm their equally fabulous content, there were wild exclamations of joy from the men – even the taciturn Wentworth. They jumped up and down, cheering, laughing and hugging Nancy and each other in a pandemonium that lasted at least two minutes. Nancy's delight, however, though considerable, was not delirious like that of the others.

As the joyous uproar subsided, she said, 'You were right all along, Nathaniel. The gold was here.'

'Sure, Captain, it's ashamed I am that I ever doubted you, me darlin' man,' cooed McMullen.

Thomas said, 'I have to admit I had doubts too, Captain – indeed I did – but you've surely made us all rich men, as you said you would.'

'Thanks be to God and to my guardian angel who guided me here,' I declared.

'Amen,' Thomas said fervently.

Cuesco now came forward, looking satisfied, if somewhat bemused, by our rapturous outpourings over what he regarded as a substance of little practical use or value.

'I am happy that you are all so pleased, sir,' he said. 'Our people are gathering together now for a short ceremony before the darkness comes. My father would like you to join us.'

'Why not?' I said, absolutely glowing from the unusual experience of being triumphant. 'They've given us all this gold, lads. Let's attend their ceremony. It's the least we can do.'

We happily followed Cuesco out into the cleared area where the entire population of the village – perhaps three hundred people – was gathered. All were standing in silence, facing the solitary house at the top, in front of which Cuesco's father sat upon a stone stool decorated with inlaid shell and gold foil. I presumed this was some kind of sacred throne. The chief wore a head-dress of multi-coloured feathers that stood upright from a broad gold band, but he was otherwise clad as I had seen him earlier. On either side of him, ten men of advanced years sat upon the ground, while on the far side of this group stood a carved stone idol, inlaid with intricate designs of gold and pearl. Its principal features were a round head with a broad mouth, circular ornaments below the ears, and two large, powerful hands.

Cuesco had positioned us only a short distance from the chief and his elders and I could not help noticing the resentful looks that many of the assembled villagers gave us when they saw we had been granted this privilege.

'I take it the idol over there is of your god, Huitzlipochtli,' I whispered to Cuesco.

'Yes, sir,' he replied. 'We made it to replace the greater one of gold and stone, passed down from our ancestors, that the Spanish took from us.'

The chief gave his son and me a long and critical look, then raised his hand towards a group of men seated beyond the idol. These were the village musicians, some of whom began to beat a repetitive rhythm on wooden drums which continued for several minutes before the others rendered a weird melody with flutes of shell or wood, punctuated by the rattle of gourds filled with pebbles. This went on for twenty minutes or more, during which time women were passing among the assembled congregation, handing out small clay bowls and filling them from earthenware jugs. When they had finished, the women bowed to the chief before intending to retire, but he berated them and with a severe expression pointed towards our party. Very sullenly, the women approached and provided each of us with a clay bowl which they filled with a murky green beverage.

'What's this swill?' Wentworth mumbled.

'Keep silent, all of you!' I commanded.

The chief gave us another long and withering glare. Then he faced his people and delivered a short speech in serious tones, after which the man to his immediate right stood up. The dark feathers of this man's head-dress inclined outwards on both sides of his head from a cotton band decorated with slender gold chains and coloured stones. He intoned a monotonous chant lasting for perhaps a quarter of an hour, after which he once more sat upon the ground.

The chief cast his eyes slowly around the congregation then raised his bowl to his lips and drank. Seeing the whole assembly doing the same, I whispered to the crew, 'Drink! Drink!'

I am unable to describe the taste of this beverage, as it was quite unlike anything I had ever tasted before. It didn't have a flavour I much enjoyed, yet it was not unpleasant. All that mattered to me at that moment was that the members of my party should be seen to be taking at least a few sips of it.

Noting that the Indians were now engaging in muted conversation, one with another, and eager to satisfy my curiosity, I quietly asked Cuesco, 'What's in this drink?'

'It's a mixture of herbs and ground, burned bones, sir,' he replied.

'Bones? What kind of bones?'

'The bones of our ancestors which we carefully preserve in a storehouse. A much respected elder died last night. Death brings chaos and disorder into our lives, so we restore harmony and order and renew the sacred bond with our ancestors by absorbing the spiritual strength of our forebears through this ceremony.'

'I see,' I said, feeling a little queasy. 'Whatever happens, don't tell any of the men what they are drinking.'

The man on the chief's right, with the dark-feathered head-dress, stood up again, raised a small bowl to his nose and sniffed it deeply.

'What's in that bowl?' I asked Cuesco.

'It's the crushed seeds of a sacred plant mixed with ground, burned shells; it enables the priest to escape from his body and journey to the land beyond the sun.'

The chief held up his hand and spoke a few words, after which the congregation began to disperse.

'Thank God that's over,' Nancy exclaimed. 'What a load of twopenny nonsense!'

'I will leave you now, sir,' Cuesco said, 'to spend the night with my family. I wish you all a sleep of comfort and pleasing dreams.'

'I'm sure we'll have that. We're used to sleeping in hammocks. After today's hard march, I've no doubt I shall sleep like a log.'

'Like a what, sir?'

'Like a log. It's an old English expression.'

Cuesco shook his head.

'Sleep like a log? It makes no sense. The English are very strange.'

With that, he departed towards his family home, on the heels of his father and others whom I presumed to be his mother, brothers and sisters. The priest, however, had seated himself upon the ornamented stool, and was still sniffing from the bowl.

The sun was setting beyond the western expanse of forest. It would be dark very soon and the accursed mosquitoes were already gathering around us for their nocturnal feast. I addressed my followers.

'We'd better turn in now, lads. I want to leave here as early as possible in the morning.'

As we turned towards our lodging house, McMullen nudged my arm.

'What in the name of the Holy Mother was all that about, Captain?'

'Your guess is as good as mine, McMullen,' I replied, considering it wisest to plead ignorance. 'Are you a Catholic, McMullen?'

'Sure, I was once, before I got more sense,' he chuckled. 'Me dear old mother would turn in her grave if she could hear me say that, so she would.'

I glanced over my shoulder as I reached the doorway of our dwelling. The priest remained alone, seated upon the stool, but had now turned to face the idol of Huitzlipochtli, constantly sniffing from his bowl beneath the darkening sky.

13

I awoke with the first light of dawn, having slept soundly in my cotton hammock despite the mosquitoes, and still feeling jubilant about the success of my venture. The means of making Corinne my bride and lifelong recipient of my eternal love was now in my hands. It was simply a question of transporting it safely back to Port Royal, and from there to London at the earliest opportunity.

Nancy still appeared to be asleep in the adjacent hammock, but the reduction in the volume of snoring suggested that some of the others were now awake. I was starting to grow quite fond of this crew – even McMullen. He was clearly a rogue, but I was beginning to trust him a little more than I had hitherto.

Suddenly, and unannounced, Indian women began to troop through the doorway, depositing calabash bowls of plantains, bananas and tortillas and earthen pots of water upon the floor. They came and went with lowered heads and without speaking.

'Breakfast!' I yelled as I rolled out of my hammock. 'Up you get, boys – and girl.'

Lofty was now up and rousing those men who were still snoring.

'Shake up your timbers, you scurvy slugabeds!' he exclaimed. 'And stuff your rum-rotted bellies!'

We were soon all seated in a semi-circle, helping ourselves to the victuals and water. Lofty sent Penryn and Ross out to feed and water the mules, tethered in the grass to one side of the building. We were all eager to be gone from this village and back to the ship, although the prospect of the intervening trek through forest and swamp was not something we relished. Penryn and Ross soon returned and resumed eating with the rest of us.

I remember that Thomas now made a friendly comment.

'I was very concerned for Nancy during that horrid slog through the swamp yesterday but, look you, she held up as well as any of us.'

'She did, to be sure,' said McMullen. 'One of the best is Nancy, so she is. There's nothing I wouldn't do for a fine girl like her.'

Nancy responded in good humour.

'Dinny imagine that all that blether will get you free drinks when we get back tae Port Royal.'

McMullen protested, 'Faith now, Nancy, I was only saying…'

He was interrupted by the sudden appearance through the small doorway of the stooped figure of Cuesco. As the young Indian straightened up, we saw that his face was grim and his eyes fearful.

'Sir, I bring very bad news,' Cuesco blurted out. 'During the night, the priest had what you would call a vision. Our chief god, Huitzlipochtli, spoke to him of his anger at our decision to give the sacred gold of our ancestors to strangers from another land. But he said that he would not punish us with floods or sickness and would allow us to honour our promise, provided the strangers presented one of their number for sacrifice.'

My stomach chilled.

'You mean Aztec ritual sacrifice?' I cried in horror.

I leapt to my feet now and the others also rose, uttering oaths as they did so.

Penryn exclaimed, 'God damn his soul! What be all this bilge this double-dealing heathen be giving us?'

'That's what I want to know, Cuesco,' I said. 'You made us a solemn promise, and now we have brought you safely home, you are breaking your word. Only a snake behaves like that. You are no longer my friend.'

'But sir, I do not break my word,' Cuesco pleaded. 'My father says you can still have the gold if you deliver up the woman for sacrifice.'

'The woman?' I exclaimed with incredulity. 'Your father wants Nancy?'

'Not my father, sir. Huitzlipochtli wants her. This is the sacred demand that he has delivered to the priest.'

Nancy stepped angrily towards him.

'Listen, you filthy savage! You can tell your pox-riddled father he can stuff Hootsyposhty up his arse! Nobody is going tae sacrifice me.'

'I strongly urge you not to tell your father that,' I said to Cuesco. 'But tell him that I am disgusted by the shame and dishonour he is bringing upon the Ahualulcos peoples, and I can give only one answer. We cannot accept such a proposal.'

'Then, sir, my father says you may all leave without fear for your lives, but the gold must remain here.'

'No!' I exclaimed. 'That will not do. We were promised the gold, so we're taking it.'

'Aye!' Lofty roared.

'By the horns of Nick, we will!' Penryn shouted.

Cuesco seemed to regain his composure now as he spoke very determinedly.

'Then, sir, I must warn you that if you attempt to do this, every one of you will die. Our warriors are many and skilled in the use of their weapons. My father is assembling them as we speak. You will not stand a chance. Instead of the woman dying and the rest of you leaving safely with the gold you came for, you will all be dead. I plead with you, sir, not to do this foolish thing.'

Taking a deep breath and endeavouring to calm down, I nodded my head.

'Very well,' I said resignedly. 'There's no other choice. We'll have to leave without the gold.'

Thomas now spoke up.

'Begging your pardon, Captain, but that is not your decision to take. In an important matter like this, look you, the decision has to be taken by all of us in council.'

'Oh, shut up, Thomas!' I exclaimed impatiently. 'We haven't got time for all that now.'

'Well now, Captain,' McMullen interposed, 'I'm thinking to meself that Taffy here has a fair point. This *is* too important to be decided by one man, so it is. There's a lot of gold at stake here.'

'But we can't possibly fight our way out of here,' I protested. 'We'd all be slaughtered.'

'That's true, beyond all doubt,' he agreed.

'So our only option is to leave without the gold,' I insisted.

'Faith, Captain, it's not our only option.'

I could hardly believe what I was hearing.

'Look!' I said with growing exasperation. 'Do you understand what Aztec ritual sacrifice entails? The priest slices open the victim's chest with a knife and cuts the heart out while it's still beating. Are you seriously suggesting we surrender Nancy to that?'

'You scurvy scum, McMullen!' Nancy cursed.

McMullen ignored her and addressed me calmly.

'Sure, Nancy probably won't suffer pain for very long. She'll lose consciousness as soon as they rip her heart out, so she will.'

'Oh, for God's sake!' I snapped. 'Surely the rest of you want nothing to do with McMullen's vile suggestion? Thomas, you were saying yesterday and again this morning how concerned you were about Nancy's welfare. Isn't that so?'

106

'Yes, Captain,' Thomas declared. 'I was concerned about Nancy and I'm still concerned; indeed I am. But, look you, we have to be practical about this matter. It is a straight choice between Nancy and the gold. Now, without Nancy, we will still be able to buy kill-devil in the Sea Horse Tavern, and even if not, we can always go to the Three Tunns or the Sugar Loaf or any of the other taverns or grog shops. And we'll have enough wealth to buy all the rum and ale we want for years to come, or perhaps to settle down with a wife and family and want for nothing. But without the gold, we will have to continue risking our necks on the account for often small returns, or else toil like slaves as merchant seamen or at some other honest labour. There seems to me to be no comparison between these two alternatives.'

'There's none denying I always said Taffy had a good head on his shoulders, so I did,' agreed McMullen.

'And if I could get my hands on a cutlass,' Nancy screamed, 'you wouldny have any kind of head on *your* shoulders, Rory McMullen, you fucking, murdering lump of dog shit!'

'Sweet Nancy,' McMullen remarked unperturbed. 'Always every inch a lady, so she is.'

'What about the rest of you?' I pleaded desperately. 'Penryn, what do you think?'

Penryn replied sourly, 'I be wanting the gold, not her. I never wanted her along in the first place.'

'Well sure, Penryn, you'd best be glad Nancy did come along,' said the Irishman. 'Otherwise, the copper-skins would have wanted one of us to be sacrificed, so they would.'

'What about you, Wentworth?' I asked.

'I be for the gold.'

'Ross?'

Ross hesitated for a moment.

'The gold. I want the gold, only … I'll be feeling bad when they kill her.'

'My father has said that the woman will not be sacrificed until you are all far enough away not to hear her screaming,' announced Cuesco.

McMullen grinned. 'Well sure, that's most considerate of him. We can't ask for fairer than that, boys, sure we can't.'

'You all make me want to vomit,' I declared. 'What kind of men are you? How can you let a woman be cruelly killed to satisfy your own greed?'

I turned to the one man present on whom I knew I could always rely.

'Lofty, for pity's sake, can you put some decency into their skulls?'

He looked at me with firm, grave eyes.

'Captain Devarre, I did most proudly sail under you and follow you into battle at Riohacha, and never doubt I'd be ready to follow you through the very gates of hell – may I choke and perish if I lie – but how I sees it is this. If we were attacking the Spaniards to seize their goods, we'd expect to lose a lot more than one person doing it, and we'd be prepared to accept that loss for a much smaller share of the loot than we be going to get from this gold. It do seem to me that one person dead be a small price to pay for what's on offer.'

The others clamoured their enthusiastic agreement.

'True as true!'

'Lofty do have the right of it!'

Above the fervent declarations, Thomas raised his voice.

'All in favour of handing over Nancy and keeping the gold, say "aye".'

'Aye!' was the resounding reply.

Nancy screamed, 'You vile bunch of mangy bilge-rats! Your mothers gave birth to you through their arseholes!

You fucking, bile-laden scum! Your stench would wrinkle the noses of pigs!'

'My sentiments exactly,' I said.

But then she turned on me.

'And you're no much better, just standing there, letting them get away with it. You gutless, lily-livered bastard! If Captain Kincaid had been here, he'd have drawn his pistols, shot one of the vermin and brought the rest intae line.'

'I daresay he would have,' I said bitterly. 'But as you never tire of telling me, Nancy, *I'm* not Captain Kincaid.'

Facing the others, I drew myself up and spoke with as much authority as I could muster.

'Enough of heated words! The decision has been agreed in council, as laid down in buccaneer law, so that's an end to it. Nancy will be delivered to the Indians and we'll be on our way. Start loading the gold onto the mules without delay; one chest on each side of the carrying harness. And be sure to fasten the chests securely with our ropes and chains. We don't want one of them falling off into the swamp.'

I turned to my boatswain.

'Lofty, take Nancy out and give her to the Indians.'

'Aye, Captain.'

Lofty stepped towards Nancy who quickly drew back from him.

'Dinny you lay a hand on me, Lofty Morris,' she snarled. 'No son of a sea hag is going tae take me to be butchered.'

'You be tough for a woman, Nancy,' he replied, 'and tougher than some men, none denying. But by God's life, you stand no chance against me. Now either you come along peaceable or I break both your arms and then take you out. How be you wanting it?'

Nancy's eyes blazed defiance and she clearly considered making a fight of it. But then her eyes suddenly calmed and shrugging her shoulders, she bowed her head.

'Take me out then,' she said, and raised her head again. 'I'm no afraid, and dinny any of you scurvy swabs think I am.'

There was a momentary silence. No one answered her, not even McMullen. Lofty pushed Nancy through the small doorway, bending double to follow her.

Cuesco said to me, 'I will go with them and tell my father of your agreement, sir.'

I followed him outside. The sun was gathering heat as it rose in the blue sky. All around, Indians began appearing from their houses. In the centre of the cleared area, around fifty Ahualulcos warriors, armed with spears, war-clubs and axes, faced our lodging. Cuesco's father and the priest stood in front, looking solemn as Lofty guided Nancy towards them, holding her firmly by the arm and accompanied by Cuesco.

The chief signalled to two of his warriors to come forward and placed one on each side of Nancy. Without speaking, Lofty turned and walked back to me. Nancy remained still and silent, her head held high but her expression anxious. Looking straight ahead, she never gave me even a glance.

Cuesco now engaged in a lengthy discussion with his father, no doubt describing the argument that had ensued before we had reached our decision. Meanwhile, my men were busy loading and securing the eight chests of gold onto our mules. The air was tense and there was no talk beyond that required while roping and chaining the chests to the saddle harnesses. Soon Lofty reported that all was ready. I checked the load of each mule in turn. All seemed secure.

'Well done, men,' I said. 'Gather up your muskets and prepare to move out.'

I turned back. Nancy was still looking straight ahead, as though I did not exist.

110

'Cuesco!' I called out. 'Can I speak to you for a moment?'

His father muttered a few words to him before the Indian hurried over.

'Sir, my father wishes me to tell you that the gods will reward you for your wise decision,' he said, 'and he wishes you a safe journey home. I wish also to say I hope we can part as friends.'

Then, swiftly drawing a pistol from my sash, I thrust the muzzle against Cuesco's chest and pulled the hammer back to full cock. My heart beat rapidly, but I spoke firmly as I looked into his startled eyes.

'Now you tell your father that we're taking the gold we were unconditionally promised and we're taking the woman also. Tell him if any of his people try to interfere, I'll kill you. I take it your people know what a pistol can do?'

'Of course, sir, yes,' he babbled. 'The Spanish – yes, they know.'

I prodded his chest with the muzzle.

'Tell your father what I said!'

Agitated Indian voices were already raised in alarm as Cuesco relayed my message to his father. The chief glared at me with furious eyes, then urgently issued clearly restraining orders to the ranks of warriors behind him who were brandishing their spears and yelling menacingly. The warriors fell silent, frustrated fury in their faces.

'Nancy!' I yelled. 'Get over here!'

Nancy started to move, but her guards seized her arms.

'Tell your father you're a dead man if he doesn't let the woman go immediately,' I threatened Cuesco.

Cuesco called to his father urgently. Without hesitation, the chief issued an instruction and the guards released Nancy who ran over to me, breathing deeply but saying nothing.

I turned and yelled to my boatswain.

'Lofty! Get the mules moving! Fast!'

111

'Begging your pardon, Captain,' Thomas said, 'but you have no right to take this action, look you, after we have reached our decision in council.'

Lofty roared, 'Be done with your prattling, Thomas, before I choke the gibbering life out of you!'

Then he addressed them all.

'Come on, you sons of poxed-up sea dogs! You heard the Captain. Get the mules on the trail double quick!'

To my great relief, the men did not hesitate but promptly led the mules off towards the forest trail by which we had come, Lofty constantly hurrying them along.

'Now, Cuesco,' I said. 'Tell your father I am taking you with me as far as our ship. Tell him you will then be released safe and sound, provided none of his people attack us or try to hinder us in any way. Any interference will result in your immediate death. Tell him!'

Cuesco relayed my words. The chief did not reply, but grimly nodded his head.

'Come on, Nancy,' I said. 'Let's be on our way.'

With my pistol prodding Cuesco's back, the three of us followed the column of mules across the clearing. Angry declamations and threatening gestures were directed at us by the warriors but, warned by their chief, none of them made any attempt to molest or pursue us, and we shortly disappeared from their view into the sheltering greenery of the forest.

14

A hundred yards or so down the trail, I caught up with the leading mule and called a brief halt. The men gathered round and began to vent their anger on my prisoner.

'Hang the heathen bastard!'

'Cleave his skull asunder!'

'Cut his throat to the bone!'

'Rip out his liver!'

'Sorry, lads,' I said. 'But we can't afford to do any of these things. Cuesco is our only guarantee that we'll reach the ship alive.'

I arranged the marching order to be the same as the previous day, with myself and Cuesco in the lead, then Nancy, followed by McMullen, and finally Thomas, Penryn, Ross and Wentworth leading the mules. Lofty would once more cover the rear and watch out for anyone who might be following us.

Nancy had remained silent and I felt too disturbed by all that had happened to say anything to her. It was only when we stopped for a rest, after marching for an hour through the dense forest, that she broke the silence between us. She had at first lain down in the shrubbery a short distance from where I was sitting with Cuesco, but now she came over and sat next to me amongst the ferns and long grass.

'I want tae thank you for saving me, Nathaniel,' she said in a humble tone I had never heard her employ during all the time I had known her. 'And I'm sorry for what I said tae you before. I should have kenned you wouldny leave me to be butchered.'

Those green eyes of hers, which I had only ever seen to be mischievous, bold or angry, were now sad and dejected. I was so surprised, I found it difficult to reply adequately.

'That's ... that's all right, Nancy. It was a stressful time for ... for all of us.'

'But I said such terrible things tae you.'

'Maybe I deserved some of them.'

'But you didny. You acted really brave back there when you saved me from thon savages.'

I nodded uncomfortably, feeling glad she believed this, but recognising that I had felt far from brave at the time.

'I was really scared, Nathaniel. I told you all I wasny, but I was. When I was handed over tae them, I was near shitting myself, even though I was determined tae brave it out.'

'It's only natural,' I said. 'I seem to have spent half my life feeling like that.'

'You dinny ken yourself, Nathaniel. You're a good man, a fine man and a gallant one.'

I looked into her eyes once more. They were shining now with absolute sincerity. I only wished I really was all of these things she now took me to be.

'But I can tell you this,' she continued bitterly. 'I'll never speak tae any of them other cold-gutted bastards as long as I live. And they winny be served any more drinks in the Sea Horse. I lay my oath tae that.'

'I suppose I can't blame you for that, Nancy.'

Just then, Cuesco turned to me and spoke gravely.

'Sir, I must speak to you. I am truly sorry you have ill feeling towards me, but I am unable to return that feeling. You saved my life and brought me back to my homeland, and I will be eternally grateful to you. I hope one day your heart will soften towards me, sir, and you will realise I had no wish that things should happen as they did. But, like my father and all of my people, I had to heed the will of Huitzlipochtli. And now, sir, as his demand has not been obeyed, I greatly fear the punishment that Huitzlipochtli will surely inflict upon my people.'

'Do you?' I replied sharply. 'Well, don't expect me to shed any tears when this happens.'

I rose to my feet.

'Come on. Get up. It's time we were moving on.'

Perhaps I was being unfair, but at that time I was in no mood to be forgiving.

We continued on our way along the trail through a tangle of trees, vines, ferns and palms, our clothing soaked with perspiration, and growing ever more weary in the stale, humid atmosphere. The heavily laden mules required frequent rests, and it took us nearly three more hours to reach the swamp. After another rest, we were soon wading knee-deep through the murky water, picking our way among the black mangrove trees and constantly stepping over their submerged roots. Nearly an hour passed before we reached the deeper swamp which gradually rose to our waists, and we once more had to find passage between the trunks and giant roots of the red mangrove trees, plagued all the while by sand flies, mosquitoes and leeches.

After struggling for another two hours through this filthy morass with the humidity at its peak, the mules appeared close to exhaustion – as indeed were we ourselves – so I called another halt. My only consolation was that, despite the arduous march having taken considerably longer than the previous day, we must now be close to the river, as Cuesco assured me we were.

We rested here, seating ourselves as best we could upon the giant mangrove roots. Once more we assumed the task of ridding our bodies of numerous leeches, while sand flies and mosquitoes buzzed and whined around us, biting our flesh repeatedly.

Sitting on a root beside me, Nancy complained in a weary voice. 'This swamp must be the Devil's shit hole. I dinny ken what I must have been thinking of when I decided tae come on this expedition. It's been an absolute unholy nightmare.'

'It certainly has,' I agreed. 'But I've always found that to be true of most so-called adventures.'

Cuesco was seated on another root a little to our left. He looked very downhearted and raised his head with little interest as McMullen waded towards him.

'My compliments to you, Cuesco,' McMullen greeted him, smiling. 'May you have a pleasant trip to hell.'

To my horror, I saw McMullen raise a pistol to Cuesco's head.

'Stop!' I cried frantically.

There was a loud report, a spurt of flame and smoke, and Cuesco toppled sideways into the swamp, his skull shattered.

'You maniac!' I screamed, dropping onto my feet in the waist-deep morass. 'What possessed you to do such a thing?'

'Sure now, Captain,' McMullen replied calmly. 'I was only giving that traitorous savage his just deserts.'

The other men were all on their feet by now and unhesitatingly acclaimed the execution.

'McMullen done right.'

'Cuesco was a split-tongued cur!'

'Damnation seize his heathen soul!'

'You fools!' I exclaimed. 'Cuesco was our shield.'

'Faith, Captain,' McMullen protested. 'We're nearly at the river, and there are no copper-skins following us, sure there aren't.'

'How can you know that?' I demanded angrily.

'Sure, Lofty hasn't spotted anyone behind us the whole way, sure he hasn't.'

116

'That doesn't guarantee that there's nobody there, you brainless chuckle-head! Indians are masters at concealing themselves in this wilderness and moving silently through it. Cuesco's father will almost certainly have sent a party to keep an unseen watch on his son and escort him safely back to the village. I have no doubt your shot will have urged them to creep closer to see if all is well.'

McMullen grinned. 'Is it that the fairies are dancing a jig in your brain, Captain? By all the saints, I must say...'

A cry from Lofty halted the Irishman's scorn.

'Indians! I did see a movement in the mangroves back there.'

There was no time to lose. I issued my orders rapidly.

'Lofty and McMullen will remain here with me. Thomas, I'm putting you in command of the others. Get Nancy and the gold back to the ship as fast as you can make the mules move. We'll hold back the Indians and follow when we can.'

'Which way, Captain?' Thomas asked, a trifle flustered.

'Straight through there! It can't be far,' I declared, pointing the direction through the mangroves.

I handed him my pocket compass, with which I had been regularly checking our route to confirm that Cuesco had not been misleading us.

'Head steadily east-north-east. Get moving!'

'Aye, Captain.'

Thomas turned and waded to his mule, while Penryn, Ross and Wentworth grasped the halters of the beasts in their charge, anxious to be on their way.

'Can I no stay with you, Nathaniel?' asked Nancy.

'Do you want the Indians to take you back for sacrifice?' I answered impatiently. 'Now, for God's sake, go!'

Thankfully, she departed without further argument. Lofty waded over to McMullen and myself. The gently arching root upon which Nancy and I had been seated

117

crossed with another, and there was a tangle of overhanging foliage from the trees on either side.

'There's pretty good cover here,' I said. 'Let's spread out a little.'

Lofty moved a few yards to the left and McMullen likewise to the right. We rested our muskets upon the roots and fully cocked the hammers, then prepared our pistols in like fashion. I peered in a semi-circle between the tree trunks and intermingled roots that lay before us across the dark swamp.

'I can't see anyone, Lofty,' I said tensely.

'Oh, they be there, Captain,' Lofty stated positively. 'I did see the foliage move down there, sure as sure.'

I glanced behind me and could faintly perceive Nancy's auburn hair and the rump of the rear mule disappearing amongst the trees and roots in that direction. Facing the front again, I prayed in a soft voice.

'Almighty and merciful God, may it please thee to strengthen our hearts, defend us against our adversaries and raise our souls up to thy Holy Kingdom should we fall. Amen.'

'Amen,' Lofty repeated.

'And may the fairies wave their magic wands and turn the heathens into pillars of salt,' McMullen jested.

Lofty snapped, 'It be your fault we be having to risk our necks, McMullen. So mind your disrespectful tongue or I'll tear it out of your bile-laden mouth!'

Hardly had these angry words been spoken when I heard a faint rustling sound behind me and the whizzing flight of a spear that thumped into Lofty's back. I gasped as my boatswain cried out and fell forward upon the giant root with the feathered shaft projecting from a spreading patch of blood between his shoulder blades. Spinning round, I raised my musket. A bronzed figure in a quilted shirt was nimbly climbing onto a root behind me, holding

118

his axe aloft. Just as he sprang forward, I took a hasty aim and pressed the trigger. The priming powder flashed and my musket discharged a shot in a billow of smoke, sending the ball smack into the Indian's chest. His face contorted as he dropped with a splash into the swamp.

The sound of another shot caused me to turn quickly as McMullen lowered his smoking musket. An Indian, still clutching a spear, was slumped over a root. As the wounded warrior struggled to raise himself, the buccaner drew his cutlass and with one hefty stroke hacked off his opponent's head. McMullen looked cautiously around him before turning to face me.

'D'you think that's all of the heathen bastards, Captain?'

'It seems so,' I said with considerable relief. 'I suppose it would only take two to keep a discreet watch on us.'

The absence of a larger pursuing force surely indicated the chief's complete faith in my word that his son would be released safe and unharmed. But just as this thought formed in my mind, a fearsome head and muscular shoulders shot upwards out of the swamp water beside me. I swung my musket butt wildly at the Indian's dripping face, but he neatly ducked aside. In near panic now, I plucked a pistol from my sash. As the warrior raised his war-club to strike, I fired a shot that knocked him backwards into the water, blood squirting from his throat.

'Beautifully done, Captain,' McMullen exclaimed. 'The crafty devil must have swum beneath the roots, so he must.'

'Indeed,' I said, aware that I was trembling slightly.

I paused and surveyed the surrounding trees and swamp. All was still and silent.

'He must be the last one, McMullen – thanks be to God.'

I replaced my pistol in my sash and laid my musket on the root before me. Wading the short distance to reach

Lofty, I grasped his hair and raised his head. The eyes were wide open and staring in that lifeless fashion with which I had become all too familiar over the years.

'Lofty's gone,' I said.

'Faith now, Captain, that's an ill-beseen shame, so it is,' McMullen said. 'But sure, every cloud has a silver lining, so they say. And seeing as poor Lofty won't be needing his two shares of the gold, there'll be all the more for the rest of us.'

I was infuriated by this statement.

'That's a foul, contemptible remark, McMullen. What a pity the Indians didn't get me! As Captain, I'll be drawing *three* shares.'

'By all the saints, Captain, that was the very thing I was thinking to meself, so it was.'

McMullen laid his musket carefully upon a root and waded slowly towards me. There was a smile on his face, but the gleam in his eyes and the rigid way he gripped his bloodstained cutlass were all the warning I required. Stepping back, I drew my own blade from its scabbard. McMullen's smile grew broader.

'Sure, there's nothing personal in this, Nathaniel. It's just a practical question of increasing my wealth. There's none denying that the lust for gold turns men into beasts, so it does.'

He surged forward and aimed a powerful blow at me. I successfully parried, following up with a thrust which he deflected as he stepped aside. But, as he raised his cutlass above his head, the blade swung into the overhead foliage and dislodged a green viper which tumbled onto his right shoulder. McMullen cried out as the serpent bit his neck, then gasped as I thrust my cutlass into his diaphragm, burying it halfway to the hilt. When I tugged my blade out, the Irishman looked at me with eyes strangely mournful.

'Oh, Nathaniel,' he said softly, 'me poor old mother would surely...'

A froth bubbled from his lips and his eyes clouded over as he toppled into the muddy water. There was no sign of the viper.

I was now overcome by a deep sadness – not just for the loss of stout and faithful Lofty, but also for my late adversary. He had often aggravated me and now he had tried to kill me, yet I had never really disliked him and I still don't dislike him as I write these words today. The lust for gold turns men into beasts, he had said. How right he was.

I swirled my bloodstained blade in the water, sheathed my cutlass and retrieved my musket from the mangrove root. Then I set off through the mangroves in what I knew to be an east-north-east direction, easily following the trail of my men by the hacked foliage that had permitted passage for the mules. My mind became dulled; I no longer heeded the leeches, mosquitoes and sand flies, nor the torrents of rain that soon descended upon me. I was aware only of my weariness as I plodded on through that fetid wilderness.

Although it seemed longer, it took me less than half-an-hour to reach the fringe of the mangroves and the smooth expanse of water of the River Tonala. With great joy I spotted the *Lady Corinne*, anchored only a hundred yards or so downriver to my left, with the last of the mules being hauled up out of the yawl onto the deck. Quite overjoyed that my men had found their way back to this spot, only a short distance from where we had landed the previous day, I waded a little way forward from the cover of the mangrove trees, drew my remaining loaded pistol and fired it into the air. A figure waved to me from the bow of the vessel. Even in the deluge of rain, I recognised it as my quartermaster, Zebediah. Once more, I experienced great joy that the Good Lord had delivered me from so many perils, and I said a prayer of thanks for that and for the successful, though costly, venture to obtain the promised gold.

It was not long before the yawl approached to pick me up. Barstow and Hershey manned the oars.

As they helped me aboard, Barstow asked with obvious concern, 'Where be the others, Captain? Do we have to wait for them?'

'No,' I solemnly replied. 'They're both dead.'

I made the same statement to Zebediah, Nancy and the others when I had clambered onto the deck of the sloop and downed the dram of rum Nancy handed to me. They gathered around, soaked to the skin, and for a moment were stunned into silence. Then Zebediah spoke, tears mingling with the rain which streamed down his chubby cheeks.

'Lofty dead? That be not suiting, Captain. I'd warrant there weren't a man in the whole world what could kill old Lofty. There be the truth of it.'

'They took him by surprise and killed him from behind,' I explained. 'I'm very sorry, Zebediah. I know you and Lofty have been mess-mates for a long time.'

'We was like brothers, none denying.'

Zebediah bowed his head and turned away.

'Begging your pardon, Captain,' he muttered and walked over to the starboard bulwark, looking through the torrents of rain towards the mangroves as though still hoping he might see Lofty coming.

'What about McMullen?' Nancy asked.

'He died bravely.'

I had made up my mind that I would allow the others to suppose McMullen had been killed by the Indians. To this day I am not quite sure why I did this. Perhaps I felt guilty about killing a shipmate, even in self-defence, but I also suspect that I was motivated by the desire to leave the others thinking well of someone who had been a generally popular member of the crew.

'Well, men,' I continued, 'we've got the gold, so let's be on our way. Up anchor! Hands to the halyards! Hoist sail!'

Zebediah was swiftly alerted from his sorrow and fully applied himself to supervising the raising of the anchor and the hoisting first of the mainsail, then the jib and stay sails. As I took my place at the tiller, Nancy grasped my arm.

'I'm so glad the heathen savages didny get you, Nathaniel.'

'Thank you, Nancy,' I said. Then, after a brief pause, 'Perhaps you could provide some kind of meal for us. God knows, we could do with it.'

She squeezed my arm and headed for the main hatch. I noticed then the eight small chests of gold deposited by the foot of the mast. They would have to be stowed away in the hold once we were properly under way. Up near the bow, our four faithful mules lay exhausted and bedraggled upon the deck. I later learned that Penryn and Wentworth had wanted to abandon the poor beasts to their fate in the swamp and forest, where they would undoubtedly have become meals for crocodiles or jaguars, but Thomas had insisted that the mules had served us well and deserved to be brought safely back to Jamaica with the rest of us.

With the north-east by east wind on our starboard bow, we had to sail close-hauled to windward as we slowly progressed downriver. I paid little heed to the driving rain. I was only grateful to be safely on board the *Lady Corinne*, heading back to Port Royal with the fortune in gold that my guardian angel had provided for me.

15

It was just after four o'clock in the afternoon that the rain ceased and the cry of alarm came from the lookout at the bow.

'A sail! A sail! Ahead and standing athwart our passage!'

I raised my spyglass to my right eye. Sure enough, at the point where the river broadened, there was a square-rigged, three-masted ship, with reefed fore and main sails, anchored with its larboard beam facing us, clearly positioned to prevent our passage to the sea.

Hershey called from the bow, 'I only did spot her when the rain did clear, Captain. Be she Spanish?'

Elevating my spyglass, I perused the red cross of Burgundy on a white field flown from fore and main mastheads.

'Yes, I'm afraid she is, Hershey,' I answered.

Lowering my spyglass, I counted eight open ports along her dark brown hull. She was a light, frigate-built vessel and undoubtedly what the Spanish called a *guardacosta*. It seemed likely we had been spotted entering the river mouth the previous morning and this guard ship had been despatched to investigate.

I promptly issued the required commands.

'Heave to! Trim your sheets!'

I put the tiller over to larboard, turning the bow to face directly windward and, with the jib and main sails adjusted to work against each other, brought the sloop to a standstill. I then summoned the crew to assemble amidships. Nancy, too, came up from below. My speech was solemn but determined.

'I'll be quite frank with you, lads. The situation we now find ourselves in is extremely grave. We're trapped by that Spanish ship. There is no way out of here except through that stretch of river ahead. So we have only one choice. We must fight our way past her.'

Zebediah cried, 'By God's blood, Captain, we'll blow them to hell!'

'Aye!' Penryn exclaimed. 'No poxy, double-damned dagos be going to take our gold from us!'

There was only one dissenting voice – Thomas.

'Let us not be too hasty now,' he said in his precise manner. 'We should surely exercise some caution here. Yonder is a ship armed with maybe twenty cannons and likely has a crew of fifty men or more. Look you, it might be wiser to parley with them and try to negotiate our way out of here.'

'Damn your blood, Thomas!' Barstow raged. 'May I burn, choke and perish if we haven't outfought bigger shit-buckets than that one in our time.'

'Aye!' Penryn concurred. 'We'll lay those dagos dead and bleeding.'

'That's the spirit, lads,' I said. 'We're buccaneers. We're not going to parley with anyone. We're going to attack!'

'But look you, Captain,' Thomas persisted. 'You must bear in mind the Governor of Jamaica's directive against anti-Spanish hostilities. We are no longer sanctioned by a privateering commission; indeed we are not. So any attack upon a ship of Spain will be regarded as an act of piracy and, look you, we may all end up dancing on the gallows.'

'Thomas, we don't have a choice,' I declared impatiently. 'We've entered Spanish waters and territory, and you can be sure the captain of that *guardacosta* intends to take us all to the nearest Spanish port in chains.'

A tirade of abuse was now directed against Thomas by the others. I held up my hand.

'Silence!' I yelled. 'We are now in a battle situation. In accordance with the articles, I expect immediate and absolute obedience from every man. Anyone failing in his duty will be instantly shot.'

There was absolute hush now. I looked around their tough, attentive faces and rather relished the power I now held over these hardy and experienced buccaneers. Believe me, dear readers, for a disgraced naval officer, second-rate portrait painter and unrequited lover, to exercise such authority was supremely satisfying.

Without further interruption, I issued my orders.

'All hammocks and chests to be stowed below. Mules to be bound and secured with ropes and chains. Powder, shot, matches, rammers and sponge tubs to be brought up on deck. All cannons to be loaded with round shot, and all muskets and pistols loaded and primed. Now, go to it, lads! Let's blast those Spanish bastards to death and damnation, and then be on our way home with our gold.'

The men gave a hearty cheer and hastened to carry out my instructions. I only hoped their fired-up enthusiasm would be maintained and that none of them – apart from Thomas – would stop to consider what a hazardous task we were about to undertake. The odds against us were undeniable: eight men and a woman opposed to a Spanish crew of fifty or more, and six three-pounder cannons to counter the fire of twenty with a likely shot weight of at least eight pounds. Yet David had prevailed against Goliath, had he not? Anyway, despite my bold words, it was my primary intention to escape with as little fighting as possible.

Nancy had remained silent and, still without a word, went off with the men to assist in the preparations for battle. Understandably embittered by their readiness to hand her over for sacrifice that morning, she had so far maintained her resolve never to speak to any of those

126

involved. She had, however, faithfully performed her duty as ship's cook, providing a meal for all half-an-hour before the sighting of the Spanish ship.

Within twenty minutes, all preparations were completed and we resumed our course downriver to meet our foe, sailing close-hauled as before. We had run out the three starboard guns, Penryn, Ross and Wentworth positioned as gunners and Thomas – whom I considered the most reliable, despite his sometimes contrary attitude – appointed to supervise and assist as required. Barstow, Hershey and Nancy stood by to man the sheets, while Zebediah remained by the tiller with me. It was my plan that we should make our escape by passing in front of the Spaniards' bow, but it was vital not to signal this intention too early. While it was imperative that we avoid being a target for the *guardacosta*'s full broadside of eight guns, if we moved off to larboard too soon, the Spanish captain would surely tack his vessel round to keep our sloop covered.

I therefore maintained our course in the middle of the river as though heading directly towards the Spanish ship in order to parley, or perhaps even surrender. Indeed, I had ordered our English colours to be lowered from the masthead to give this very impression and sent Hershey forward to the bow to observe whatever preparations the Spanish might be making.

'Captain,' said Zebediah suddenly, 'd'you suppose Captain Kincaid might be looking down from them clouds up in heaven and urging us on to give the dagos a good drubbing?'

'Indeed he might be, Zebediah,' I answered positively, even though I had grave doubts that Jonathon Kincaid would have been permitted entry into God's Kingdom.

Zebediah began to sing a shanty I had never heard before and, to my delight, the others displayed their sustained spirit by joining in:

My name was Jon Kincaid when I sailed, when I
  sailed.
My name was Jon Kincaid when I sailed.
My name was Jon Kincaid when for plunder I did
  raid,
And dear the Spaniards paid when I sailed, when I
  sailed,
And dear the Spaniards paid when I sailed.

We were now drawing dangerously close. I could see
the dark muzzles of the Spaniards' cannons poking
menacingly in our direction from their opened gun ports.

    Hershey shouted, 'I do see wisps of smoke, Captain.'

    'They've lit their matches,' I said hastily to Zebediah, as
I pushed the tiller hard over to starboard, turning our bow
towards the mangroves along the west bank of the river.

    Zebediah yelled, 'Make sail! Loosen sheets!'

    Barstow and Nancy slackened the sheets in order to
sail downwind and Hershey now hastened to assist them.
The wind, on our starboard quarter, began to fill our
sails and we sped westwards just as the *guardacosta*'s
broadside of heavy guns thundered out, belching flame
and smoke. But only one cannon ball struck the *Lady
Corinne*; it smashed the lantern at our stern.

    'Barstow!' I yelled. 'Run up our flag!'

    The red cross of Saint George on its white field was
promptly hoisted and fluttered proudly from our masthead.

    'Now we've got something to fight under, boys!' I called
out. 'God bless England!'

    'And Wales!' exclaimed Thomas indignantly.

    'And Scotland!' added Nancy.

    Hershey regularly sounded the depth of the river with
a lead line, but with our shallow draft we had no reason
to worry. As we neared the mangroves, I put the tiller
over to larboard to turn downriver again.

Zebediah yelled, 'Trim sheets for close-haul!'

With the sheets trimmed and the wind once more on our starboard bow, I issued a further order.

'Thomas! Have your men light their matches and depress the guns to fire low.'

The gunners assisted one another to raise the breeches of the guns with handspikes, adjusting the quoins on the wooden carriages so that the cannon muzzles pointed downwards. We soon reached the point where the river broadened, the bowsprit and prow of our foe looming ever larger meanwhile on our starboard bow. Belatedly, the Spaniards had now hauled up their anchor and were loosening their sails.

'Thomas!' I called. 'Each gun to fire low into the hull as we sail past.'

'Aye, Captain!' Thomas responded.

Penryn, Ross and Wentworth blew upon their smouldering matches and stood by the breeches of their guns. The planking of the *guardacosta*'s bow was now little more than five yards distant from our starboard beam.

'Now, Thomas!' I yelled.

'Number one gun, fire!' Thomas ordered. 'Number two, fire! Number three, fire!'

One by one, the gunners applied their matches to the powder behind the touch-holes and the guns discharged in rotation, their depressed barrels sending round shot smashing into the timbers below the enemy's waterline amidst clouds of rising smoke. The gunners had leapt aside as each cannon recoiled. Almost simultaneously, the Spaniards' two bow chasers had opened fire, but these guns were too elevated for this close range and their shots passed harmlessly over our heads, though tearing one hole in the mainsail.

But a greater danger now threatened. Spanish musketeers, wearing steel *morion* helmets, dark blue coats and leather bandoliers, were massed on the forecastle. They were well positioned to deliver a deadly, concentrated fire with their smoking matchlock muskets as our hull ceased to be obscured from their view by the sails of their bowsprit and emerged beyond their starboard bow. With a roaring discharge of gunpowder smoke, a veritable storm of shot swept across our starboard bulwark. Momentarily frozen by the horror of it all, I heard Thomas scream as he grasped at his head and chest, while Penryn, Ross and Wentworth reeled and convulsed from the impact of multiple musket balls before, like Thomas, they fell writhing to the deck.

'Muskets! Muskets!' I screamed. 'Get those bastards on the forecastle!'

Zebediah, Barstow and Hershey hastened to our starboard bulwark and opened fire with their long-barrelled flintlocks upon the Spanish musketeers now busily reloading on the forecastle. Like most buccaneers, my men were expert marksmen and to my unashamed delight, I saw three Spaniards go down.

A Spanish officer, wearing a plumed hat and clutching a smoking pistol, pressed forward from his men.

'*Asesinos ingléses!*' he yelled. '*Cobardes!*'

(English murderers! Cowards!)

I called back, '*Canalla española! Hijos de putas!*'

(Spanish rabble! Sons of whores!)

Holding the tiller steady with my left hand, I discharged my pistol at him and saw blood spread across his face as he fell. My three remaining men had now grabbed the muskets of the dead gunners and with these fired a second volley. Even at the increasing distance, at least two more of the Spanish musketeers appeared to be hit. My satisfaction was further enhanced when I heard cries of alarm from the Spanish vessel and observed her sudden forward tilt.

Zebediah turned to me, beaming with delight.

'She be going down, Captain. Praise be to God, we must have done serious damage below the waterline. She be going down by the bow.'

We cheered ecstatically. We may have killed only a few of the Spanish with our musket fire, but a good number more would surely drown. Some readers may be shocked by such callous delight at the prospect of so many poor souls going to their deaths, but I say unto them that if they are ever in a battle in which brothers-in-arms are slaughtered before their eyes, they will find that the greater the revenge, the sweeter it feels. It is only later that those with a conscience are inclined to be tormented by guilt and remorse. As I trust my readers will have learned by now, I am one such person.

Zebediah inspected the four bodies sprawled around the three starboard cannons.

'They all took several hits, Captain,' he reported calmly. 'Shot to pieces they be – every one. God rest their souls.'

'We'll wait until we're out to sea before we give them burial,' I replied grimly.

And so we made our escape. As we continued downriver, the *guardacosta* sank ever lower in the water behind us, gradually at first, then more rapidly. Two small boats were being rowed back and forth between the sinking ship and the swamp-free greenery of the east bank. I saw a few figures swimming in the water, but I had little doubt that many of the Spanish crew would be unable to swim and would consequently drown. On the last occasion I looked back I saw only the mizzen top disappearing below the surface.

Darkness had fallen when, being well out to sea, I decided to heave-to. By lantern light, the remnant of my crew assembled amidships where the blood-stained bodies of Thomas, Penryn, Ross and Wentworth had been laid side by side at the starboard bulwark.

'Remove caps,' I commanded.

The men respectfully complied. I then briefly recited what I could recall of the prayer for burial at sea. 'We therefore commit these bodies to the deep to be turned into corruption, looking for the resurrection of the body when the sea shall give up her dead, and the life of the world to come, through our Lord Jesus Christ. Amen.'

'Amen,' the three men repeated. Nancy remained silent.

'Into the water with them, boys,' Zebediah ordered.

Barstow and Hershey, both deserters from the King's Navy and of robust build, then slung the bodies, one by one, into the sea.

'Now that sad duty is done, lads, we'll get the ship under way,' I said, replacing my hat. 'We surely deserve a few good draughts of kill-devil tonight.'

'That be what we all be needing, Captain, sure as sure,' agreed Zebediah. 'We'll toss a hearty pot to the bloody shirts of all the boys what we lost, afloat and on shore.'

'And to the gold what we got,' added Barstow.

'Aye,' Hershey exclaimed. 'And don't forget we all be going to get bigger shares now there be only a few of us.'

'Glory be, that be so!' Barstow rejoiced.

I suppressed my anger at their heartless attitude and sternly issued my orders.

'Man the sheets! Close-haul to windward!'

As the men dispersed, I returned to the tiller. Nancy followed me and I discerned the brightness of her eyes in the flickering light of the nearby lantern.

'I didny say amen tae your prayer,' she said. 'I hope the evil bastards roast in hell!'

Before I could think of a suitable reply, she spoke again.

'Nathaniel, dinny you think it's uncanny that the only men killed were the ones that went with us tae the Indian village? Maybe Hootsyposhty was taking revenge for no getting his sacrifice.'

132

'Then, why would Huitzlipochtli have spared us?' I queried. 'No, Nancy. It's just an odd coincidence.'

She shook her head. 'I'm no so sure. Maybe he's saving us for later.'

16

Long and laborious were the hours during our voyage back to Jamaica, Barstow and I on larboard watch, alternating with Hershey and Zebediah on starboard. Nancy helped as best she could, in addition to her cooking duties. It was a harmonious trip. In truth, we were too busy to quarrel, and the two former naval seamen had not yet lost the habit of immediate obedience to command.

Never able to sail before the wind, most of our time was spent tacking alternately to windward and leeward with the veering north-east by north to north-east by east winds on our larboard bow or beam. We had consequently been at sea for ten days before we finally moored at a wharf in Chocolata Hole, Port Royal, in the late evening of Thursday, 22 July 1669.

Our arrival aroused little interest. The two customs officials who came on board knew Nancy well and greeted her genially. It would be clear to them that a small sloop, with only the female owner and a crew of four aboard, could not have been indulging in piratical activities, and they had no reason to doubt Nancy's story that she had taken an old friend from London on a cruise around the coast of the island. Indeed, they didn't trouble themselves to search the hold where our small chests of gold were concealed in barrels of remaining foodstuffs.

After a large dram of rum and an exchange of ribald gossip with Nancy, they went on their way in high spirits.

Our own morale was even higher that night as I divided our shares of the gold bars: three shares for me, two for

Zebediah and one each for Barstow, Hershey and Nancy, as agreed in our articles. There was no bickering. The calculation was perfectly simple. There was a total of eight shares to pay and we had eight chests of gold. It couldn't have been better.

When Zebediah went ashore and shortly returned with a hired coach and Nancy's own carriage, we departed from the *Lady Corinne* well content. Once the chests were loaded, Barstow and Hershey climbed into the coach, but Zebediah hesitated.

'Captain Devarre,' he said solemnly. 'I be proud to have sailed with you once more. And it be in my mind now that Captain Kincaid were only a cat's whisker better than you, bless your heart.'

I shook his hand.

'And I couldn't have asked for a better quartermaster, Zebediah,' I responded. 'Thank you.'

Seeming very moved, he climbed into the coach. I joined Nancy upon the red velvet seat within her plush conveyance, and off we went up Fisher's Row. The night was illuminated by the external lanterns and interior candles of the many taverns and other drinking dens, all of which were enjoying their customary nocturnal trade. Snatches of song and guffaws of laughter filled the air from the verandahs and open windows.

'It's good tae be home,' Nancy said.

'Yes it is,' I agreed. 'There were times in Tabasco when I thought we'd never see Port Royal again.'

'I'll arrange for someone tae look after the sloop and the mules until I can sell them. Anyway, if they got stolen, I wouldny really care.'

'I suppose not, now you have your share of the gold.'

'I dinny want the gold, Nathaniel. You can add my share tae your own.'

I looked at her quite amazed.

'But you're entitled to it, Nancy, after all you've been through.'

'It's precisely because of what I've been through that I dinny want it. The whole episode was horrid – hateful. I dinny want tae be reminded of it. And I have a bad feeling about the gold. I believe it has brought us bad luck and will do so again.'

'The curse of Huitzlipochtli?' I asked with a smile.

'You can laugh if you want tae, Nathaniel,' she answered grimly. 'But I'm really serious about this. I dinny want that devil-cursed gold. Anyway, what would I want it for? I'm already earning more money from the tavern than I ken what tae do with, and I couldny possibly retire and try tae live like a fine lady, socialising with all thon snobbish wives of the merchants and assembly members. It just wouldny be me and I'd be bored tae death. I love the Sea Horse. I'd never want tae leave it. And you said you wanted a fortune tae marry this Lady Corinne doxy. So you take my gold tae add tae your own, and go ahead like the stupid jackass you are and buy yourself a snooty, money-grabbing wife. You've got no more brains than a sea-turtle!'

I was completely taken aback by this outburst.

'I'm sorry, Nathaniel,' she added hastily before I could reply. 'I shouldny have said that. You saved my life and I'll be forever grateful for that. I really want you tae have my gold, and I hope it brings you happiness.'

'Very well, Nancy,' I said, bemused. 'If that's really what you want, I'll gratefully accept your kind offer.'

'Believe me, Nathaniel, you're welcome tae the murderous, evil stuff.'

We were now in Queen Street and soon arrived at the Sea Horse Tavern which we entered through a private door in an alley at the side. The four small chests were carried up to Nancy's room and deposited for safekeeping in her money chest – a great trunk with a double lock.

136

I saw little of Nancy for the rest of that night. She completely immersed herself in checking that all had gone well in her absence and was busy with stocktaking and accounting until a very late hour. Her Negro boy brought a supper of lobsters, crabs and manatee flesh, together with a pitcher of beer and another of kill-devil, to my room, and I retired early to bed.

Lying there in the darkness, trying to ignore the mosquitoes and the constant hum of voices from below, I found my thoughts were all of Corinne. Now that the fortune I had obtained for my Lady was secured, it was imperative I transport it to London as soon as possible. I felt some concern that the gold might somehow be discovered and stolen, but my greatest fear was that I might arrive home too late and find Corinne already married. I tried to reassure myself that my guardian angel would provide me with a successful outcome. Had he not ensured that everything had gone according to plan up to now? And had not Corinne been convinced that it would take her a long time to find a rich husband who would be prepared to overlook her age and reputation? I also reminded myself of her belief that she would probably be required to accept someone who would not be her ideal choice of husband – apart, that is, from his wealth.

Clearly, I *had* to return with my fortune at the earliest possible moment – as much for my darling Corinne's sake as for mine.

Thus resolved, the following morning I lost no time in proceeding to the deep-water harbour beyond Thames Street, where, to my delight, I learned that the *Jamaica Merchant* would be sailing for London that very evening. I promptly boarded the vessel and spoke to Stephen Gage, captain and part-owner, who informed me he would be happy to provide me with a berth aboard. Yet again, I was aware of the guiding hand of my guardian angel and extended my gratitude in prayer to the Almighty.

In the carriage on the way to the harbour late that afternoon, Nancy was strangely silent. Whenever I spoke, she would merely nod or reply with brevity. I did not know what to make of it, yet it seemed to fit the pattern of obscure but undeniable changes in her behaviour since the disturbing incident at the Indian village.

Her mood remained the same when we were standing on the quay before the three-masted, square-rigged *Jamaica Merchant*. Negroes carried sacks and chests up the gangplank, while others unloaded carts or toiled across the jetty with crates from the massive warehouses behind us. A team of Negro porters waited patiently beside my four small, and now padlocked, Spanish chests and my medium-sized sea-chest until I was ready to board.

'Here we are again, Nancy,' I said, forcing a smile. 'Do you remember how we stood on this very quay when I went home last year?'

In her white-plumed, red velvet hat and pink satin, silver-laced gown, Nancy looked magnificent as always, despite her anxious expression as she grasped my forearm.

'I dinny want you tae go, Nathaniel,' she declared desperately. 'Bide a wee while longer. Please!'

'But I've got to go, Nancy,' I replied, bemused by this unexpected plea. 'I've paid for my passage.'

'What does that matter? Dinny go. Stay with me. I need you.'

I could hardly believe it. Her green eyes were bright with tears.

'Can you no understand what I'm saying tae you, Nathaniel? I want you tae fuck me.'

Now my credulity was being stretched to the limit.

'You what?'

'I do. I really do. I canny explain it. It's just – well –

after all we went through together and the way you saved me from the savages, I began tae see you differently.'

'Why didn't you tell me this last night?' I demanded angrily.

'Och, I was too busy last night sorting things out in the tavern. I didny have time tae think about anything else. Anyway, I didny ken it last night. It's only just dawned on me today since you told me you were leaving.' She shook her head. 'I dinny ken what's happening tae me. I've never felt like this in my life before. You canny leave me like this. You've got tae fuck me, Nathaniel. You've got tae!'

I glanced at the lovely, bulging flesh above the silver lace of her bodice and then into her tear-filled eyes.

'I'm sorry, Nancy,' I said, gently but firmly. 'I've always been desperate to ... to take you to bed, as you well know, but my guardian angel guided me to this prompt passage home and I've got to go. I can't risk delaying my departure. Time is vital to my purpose. I've told you before.'

She squeezed my arm and persisted.

'Och, Nathaniel, you'll be going home tae someone who doesny really want you – only lots of money. If it's a wife you want, I'll marry you. We can be married in D'Oyley's oak church. I ken John Maxwell, the minister, well. He calls me a sinner, but he likes me because I'm Scottish like him. I'll be a dutiful wife tae you, because I've always wanted tae be truly regarded as respectable. And I promise you, Nathaniel, I'll keep my legs closed tae everyone except you.'

Nancy delivered this remarkable declaration, hardly pausing to take breath. Needless to say, I had grown more astounded with each sentence. Completely disorientated, I could not make a suitable reply. I was aware only of the need to extricate myself from this situation.

'Goodbye, Nancy,' I blurted out. 'I'm sorry.'

I wrenched my arm free from her grasp and signalled to the waiting Negro porters.

'Let's go!' I said sharply.

As I walked swiftly towards the *Jamaica Merchant*, my mind was in turmoil. This abrupt and unhappy parting was the last thing I wanted, but I couldn't bear to be with Nancy a moment longer. There were so many things I should have said to her in farewell. I should have told her how grateful I was for her unforeseen endearments. I should have said how much I would miss her, and I certainly should have emphasised to her how much I wanted to ... to...

Oh, don't even think about it, I told myself frantically. You'll drive yourself crazy!

At the top of the gangplank, I looked back across the quay. Nancy's red and gold carriage, drawn by two white horses, was already turning into Thames Street. She had not waited to wave goodbye as she had done the previous year.

I could hardly blame her for that.

17

The *Jamaica Merchant* moored at Butolph's Wharf, just to the east of London Bridge, shortly before noon on Wednesday, 22 September 1669. Custom-house officers promptly swarmed on board. After carefully inspecting my four small chests of gold bars, two of these officers claimed almost half the contents of one of them as the ten per cent import duty owed to the King and issued me with a receipt upon which was stated that an unspecified amount of money would be refunded to me in due course. The fellows seemed professional and honest to me, so I was prepared to accept this outcome – not that I had much choice.

Once ashore, I hired a hackney carriage and two porters and proceeded without delay to the extensive premises of Alderman Edward Backwell, goldsmith-banker, in Lombard Street. There, I was admitted to the office of Mr Crawley – a plump, jolly individual with whom I normally dealt regarding my inheritance from my father and my own small earnings from painting. He examined the contents of my four chests and weighed a bar from each of them, from time to time making notes with his quill pen on a sheet of paper upon his desk. Then, he sat down at the desk and invited me to sit opposite him.

'My, my, Mr Devarre,' he said brightly. 'Where did you get that lovely lot?'

'I've just returned from Jamaica,' I cautiously explained, 'where I had some good luck.'

'Good luck? I'll say you did! Been back to the old piracy game, eh?'

'You could say that,' I said, feeling pleased that – unlike many other people – Mr Crawley was prepared to believe I had been a pirate in my time. 'How much is it all worth, Mr Crawley?'

'Well, I'll have to have the bars properly assayed, but my present estimate is that you have at least fifteen thousand pounds' worth there.'

'Fifteen thousand?' I exclaimed. 'That's quite a fortune, isn't it?'

'A fortune?' he echoed, his plump face beaming. 'By God, sir, it certainly is! I maintain a home, a wife and three children quite comfortably on an income of fifty pounds a year. If I had that gold, it would keep me going for...' he hesitated a moment. 'By God, sir, for three hundred years! You'll never have to work again, Mr Devarre, or listen to any more complaints from your customers.'

He laughed merrily at his quip. I laughed with him.

'Mind you,' he continued, 'my wife loves that portrait you painted of her. You didn't make her look half as fat and ugly as she really is.'

He now positively bellowed with laughter, hammering on the desk with his clenched hand.

So I departed from the offices in Lombard Street with a light heart. My fortune in gold was safely deposited and I intended to lose no time in conveying the glad tidings to Corinne. Now she could marry someone whom she would be pleased to have as a husband – someone who possessed enough wealth to keep her in comfort and security for the rest of her life. This was going to be a happy day for both of us, and I could be sure she would not wait until night before taking me to her bed. It would be like old times, only better, because now I would have the added joy of knowing we were to be wed.

Once more in a hackney carriage, I was borne westwards along the busy thoroughfares of Cheapside, Paternoster

Row, Ave Maria Lane, Ludgate Street, Ludgate Hill, Fleet Street, The Strand, Charing Cross and Pall Mall, until finally arriving in St James's Square. Bearing my sea-chest, containing nothing of any great weight, upon my shoulder and in a state of rising excitement, I was admitted to the Malvor mansion and directed to the parlour. Corinne's steward, Matheson, shortly hastened into the room. He was a well-built man in his mid-forties with receding dark hair.

'Why, Mr Devarre,' he exclaimed with enthusiasm. 'A pleasure to see you again, sir. Been killing any more papists lately?'

'Indeed, I have, Matheson,' I replied with a smile, being long used to his bigotry, which was no worse than most people's. 'I've just returned from the Spanish Main where we shot and drowned a goodly number.'

'Well, that is music to my ears, sir. May the Good Lord reward you.'

'Is her Ladyship at home?' I keenly enquired.

'Why no, sir. She's gone to get married.'

For a moment I froze. This shattering news could not possibly be true.

'You jest, of course, Matheson,' I uttered clutching at a straw.

'No, sir. She really is. She's getting married to Sir Roger Trevanyon in St Martin-in-the-Fields.' As I struggled to accept this information, Matheson continued, 'I wish it was you she was marrying, Mr Devarre. You was our favourite of all 'er Ladyship's men friends, and there's the truf of it – apart from Mr Darby, that is.'

At last focusing my attention upon the reality of the situation, I realised I must not give up – not after all I had been through. Corinne *had* to be mine!

'What time is the wedding?' I demanded.

'Free o'clock, sir.'

I pulled my watch from my waistcoat pocket and opened the lid. The time was a quarter to three.

'Matheson, can you provide me with a horse, fast?'

'Of course, Mr Devarre, sir. My pal, Robbins, will 'ave one saddled for you in the shake of a tail.'

Ten minutes later, I was seated astride a fine bay horse, galloping along Pall Mall and swerving dangerously around carriages, carts and sedan chairs. Startled strollers at the roadsides turned their heads and one of them yelled jocularly, 'Watch out! The Devil's right behind you!' I paid him no heed. All I knew was that I had to get to the church before it was too late to save Corinne from the ills of an unsuitable marriage and attain my heart's desire. In my plain green velvet coat and plumed hat, I was no doubt poorly attired to attend an aristocratic wedding, but then I was hardly an invited guest.

The tower of the Church of St Martin-in-the-Fields loomed clearly ahead of me. I sped onwards, traversing the crossroads of Charing Cross and turning left into St Martin's Lane. I steered my horse between two of the carriages waiting outside the church and reined in before the oak doors.

Leaping from my horse, I hastily tied the reins around a post and dashed through the entrance, across the darkened vestibule and into the church. Some people seated in the rear pews looked round at me curiously, but my attention was focused upon the scene at the end of the central aisle.

There, before the high altar, was my darling Corinne in her white bridal gown, her blonde top-knot and ringlets visible through her fine lace veil, standing beside a broad-shouldered gentleman in a lilac-coloured coat. I presumed the elderly man, leaning on a cane, to Corinne's left was the bride's father. Corinne had told me little about him, other than that he resented her notoriety and only rarely invited her to the family home. A richly attired younger man stood on the groom's right, and the Anglican minister, in flowing surplice, faced the couple, prayer book in hand. The pews on both sides of the aisle were filled with grandly dressed persons, but I hardly noticed them or the others crowding the galleries.

Almost overcome by relief and apprehension, I realised I had arrived just in time as the minister began to speak.

'Dearly beloved, we are gathered here in the sight of God, and in the face of this congregation, to join together this man and this woman in holy matrimony, which is an honourable estate, instituted by God...'

I looked again at the groom. As far as I could tell, he looked close to forty years old. Sir Roger Trevanyon – I'd heard the name before but knew nothing about him. I wondered how Corinne had managed to ensnare him, despite her well-known reputation.

The minister's voice droned on.

'...and therefore is not by any to be enterprised, nor taken in hand, unadvisedly, lightly or wantonly, to satisfy men's carnal lusts and appetites, like brute beasts that have no understanding; but reverently, discreetly, advisedly, soberly...'

Was it Sir Roger's carnal lust for her that Corinne had played upon? After all, she was an exceedingly appetising woman. Had she perhaps refused his gratification without a wedding ring? And had he abandoned all reasoned arguments against marrying 'the Dishonourable Lady Trollop of St James's Square', as Corinne was known in Whitehall, driven mad by desire for her?

'...was ordained for a remedy against sin, and to avoid fornication; that such persons as have not the gift of continence might marry, and keep themselves undefiled...'

But would he refrain from adulterous conduct once he had satisfied his lust for her? And was it not likely that he might be a drunkard, an addictive gambler or a wife-beater – traits displayed by the nobility every bit as much as the common man? Corinne deserved better than that.

'... for the mutual society, help and comfort that the one ought to have of the other, both in prosperity and adversity. Into which holy estate these two persons present come now to be joined. Therefore if any man can show any just cause why they may not lawfully be joined together, let him now speak, or else hereafter for ever hold his peace.'

'I can show just cause!' I yelled excitedly.

With many gasps and shocked utterances, all heads turned as I strode down the central aisle. My heart was racing (and I was indeed amazed at my audacity) as I passed the six startled bridesmaids.

'Because Lady Corinne Malvor would rather marry me,' I declared loudly to the astonished minister, halting before the bride and groom who had swung round to face me.

'Nathaniel!' Corinne exclaimed in great surprise, though not in anger. 'What on earth do you think you're doing?'

She was a vision of beauty in her richly embroidered white silk gown. I looked into her blue eyes and ardently declared, 'Corinne, you told me once I was the person you would most want to marry if only I had a fortune. Well, I now *have* a fortune. I've just returned from the New World with fifteen thousand pounds in gold.'

'Oh Nathaniel, you are a silly boy,' Corinne chided. 'Fifteen thousand pounds? Roger is worth at least five times that amount, *and* he has a title.'

'Corinne, who is this fellow?' Sir Roger demanded.

'This is an old friend of mine, Roger – Mr Nathaniel Devarre.' Corinne introduced me with remarkable calm. 'He's a painter and a pirate – a jolly nice chap but inclined to be foolish at times.'

Gently pushing Corinne to one side, Sir Roger faced me squarely. The profusion of ginger curls which formed his periwig matched the colour of his moustache and goatee beard. His features were strong and handsome, and his lilac silk chamlet coat was extravagantly trimmed with gold and silver lace.

'Your behaviour is outrageous, sir!' he declared. 'How dare you come here disrupting our holy nuptials?'

Corinne grasped Sir Roger's arm as though to restrain him and addressed me gently.

'Nathaniel, whatever I may have said to you was no doubt true at that time, but I never expected then I would ever meet someone like Roger. I love Roger with all my heart and soul and I could never marry anyone but him. Now please leave, Nathaniel; there's a good boy.'

I was stunned by her words. The dream I had nurtured over the past months was shattered. The goal I had striven for, suffered for, killed for and sacrificed men's lives for, had been just that – merely a lovesick fool's forlorn dream.

I looked towards the elderly minister, who appeared to have been shocked into silence.

'I apologise for interrupting your service, reverend sir,' I said.

'Just go!' he responded sharply.

Turning to Corinne, I added, 'I'm sorry, Corinne. I'll never trouble you again.'

Sir Roger's fury, however, had not abated.

'Being sorry cannot excuse your disgraceful conduct, sir, nor can it wipe away the insult to my honour, nor to that of my bride. I challenge you now to meet me on the field of honour, thereby to –'

'Oh Roger!' Corinne interrupted him impatiently. 'That really isn't necessary.'

'I assure you that it is, Corinne,' he replied. 'After such abominable behaviour by this ill-mannered blackguard, I'd be despised and scorned for the rest of my life if I failed to teach the lout a lesson.'

'I willingly accept your challenge, Sir Roger,' I declared.

'That is well,' Sir Roger said, growing calmer. 'My bride and I will be departing for Paris at noon tomorrow, and I am not prepared to wait until after our honeymoon to obtain satisfaction. We'll meet at dawn tomorrow in St James's Park.'

Corinne exclaimed, 'But what about *my* satisfaction, Roger? What about our wedding night?'

'That will have to be cut short, my love. This other matter cannot be delayed.'

He turned back to me.

'Owing to the shortage of time, I suggest we dispense with seconds and all unnecessary formalities. I will arrange for a trusted doctor, with considerable experience in duelling matters, to be present. That is all we shall require. Are you agreed?'

'Agreed,' I replied.

'One thing more, sir. I received a musket ball in my knee at Worcester, back in fifty-one, and am no longer sufficiently agile for swordplay. I know it is unusual, but would you have any objection to pistols?'

'Pistols?' I shook my head. 'No, I'd have no objection.'

'I'm obliged to you, sir,' he said politely. 'Do you know where the rows of trees intersect above the eastern end of the canal?'

'Yes, I know the spot.'

'We shall meet there at dawn tomorrow. I bid you good day.'

As I turned to walk back up the aisle, I was conscious that all eyes in the congregation were upon me, while a buzz of excited chatter arose from all around. I had not taken many steps, however, when I heard Corinne's voice.

'Nathaniel!'

I halted and turned as she hastened to my side, the long train of her gown trailing behind her and causing some consternation amongst the bridesmaids.

'Nathaniel, I never held you responsible for killing Frederick, as he brought that upon himself. Nor did I blame you for killing my brother-in-law, Darby, as he surely deserved his fate. But if you now kill Roger – the only man I've ever really loved – I will never forgive you for it. Never!'

I looked into her blue eyes, longing to hold her naked in my arms once more.

'Goodbye, Corinne,' I said, and briefly kissed her on the lips, causing gasps from the pews on either side. Our eyes met again in a moment of mutual affection and sorrow, before we turned to go our separate ways.

I hurried out of the church into the dull daylight beneath an overcast sky. The bay horse, tethered to the post, turned slightly and looked at me. I threw my arms around his sturdy neck and wept.

18

I was comfortably accommodated that night in one of the well furnished rooms of the prosperous King's Head Inn, Charing Cross. A year or so before, I had painted a portrait of the innkeeper, Peter Griffith, a wealthy bachelor, who was not dissatisfied with the completed work. He had since welcomed me as a guest whenever I had the need to stay overnight in London and wasn't seeing Corinne. However, I normally ate dinner there for one shilling, seated at the second table, rather than paying two shillings and sixpence for the privilege of sitting at the host's table.

Understandably, I was not very hungry that night and ate only a meagre supper in one of the small private rooms beyond the bar. A cheery fire burned in the grate and the oak table was well polished. A serving wench brought me venison pasties and Woodstreet cake, in addition to two quarts of Northdown ale, and a pint of sack. I knew I should be refraining from imbibing too much strong drink in order to keep myself in the best possible shape for the following morning's ordeal, but I had grown more and more depressed as the enormity of the disaster that had befallen me loomed ever larger in my mind.

By the time I got round to drinking the sack, I was plagued by guilt for the fate of those who had fallen victim to my folly. Lofty, McMullen, Thomas, Penryn, Wentworth, Ross, Cuesco, three other Ahualulcos Indians and an unknown number of Spanish mariners had forfeited their lives as a result of my insane passion for a beautiful woman and my unreasoning determination to obtain a fortune with which to purchase her hand in marriage. And what had been achieved? Nothing! It had all been for nothing. Corinne had married someone else that very afternoon, and now I was required to risk my life in a duel with a stranger from which I had nothing whatsoever to gain.

When I had earlier returned to the Malvor mansion in order to bring back the bay horse and collect my sea-chest, Matheson had not hesitated to offer his advice.

'Do for the bastard, Mr Devarre,' he had said. 'Then you can maybe get together again wiv 'er Ladyship.'

Regrettably, that option was not open to me. I had no doubt at all that Corinne would remain committed to her declaration that she would never forgive me if I were to kill Sir Roger. The previous year, I had killed Darby Malvor and consequently bedded Corinne; there was no possibility of history repeating itself.

As I left the private room to make my way unsteadily up to bed, my attention was drawn to a bearded young man, seated upon a stool in the corner by the bar, who was strumming a mandolin as he sang a doleful, ancient ballad:

> ...And so I cry, love come back to me,
> For thou art the cause of my mis-er-y.

Thus the song ended. Nobody applauded, only I. The young man looked over and solemnly nodded to me. Seized by a sudden, drunken rage, I turned towards the guests seated at the scattered tables and, swaying back and forth, I gave vent to my feelings.

'What's the matter with you all? Have you no ear for a rendering of the cruel ravages of love? Have your souls

151

never been in anguish? Have your hearts never been broken? Have your bitter tears never ... never flowed...?'

I broke off and looked round at the awe-struck faces of the now silent guests. I wasn't so drunk that I was unable to realise I was making a fool of myself.

'I ... I am sorry ... ladies and gentlemen,' I said jerkily. 'I ... I do apologise.'

I turned and headed for the staircase, feeling wretched. The guests immediately resumed their chatter, and, to give them their due, whatever they may have said to each other, none called out any unkind remarks in my wake.

Those readers who assume I did not sleep well that night are absolutely correct. I slept deeply for perhaps three hours, then fitfully for a while, at the end of which I dreamt of Harriet's bones scattered on the river bank and woke up in a cold sweat. After that, I dared not try to sleep again.

At five o'clock on that fateful Thursday morning, I departed from the inn, unshaven and without sustenance and weary of body and mind. Indeed, I felt positively ill. In the darkness, relieved only by light from the occasional lanterns hanging outside the entrances of buildings, I walked to the other side of Charing Cross into King Street and turned past the boundary wall of Wallingford House into St James's Park. I then headed southwards in almost total darkness, with a line of oak trees on my right and the Spring Garden on my left. During this march to an unknown destiny, I endeavoured not to think about anything, a task not difficult for my weary mind. I was, however, acutely aware of the fear gnawing in the pit of my stomach.

The whinnying of a horse came to me on the light morning breeze as I continued over the dew-soaked grass. After crossing a narrow footpath, I soon arrived at the final tree in the row. From here, I turned right, adjacent to another curving row of oak trees and, as the sky began to lighten in the east, I spotted two cloaked figures ahead of me, standing beside a small, two-horse carriage on the other side of another footpath.

As I approached them, noting that my adversary appeared to have an excessive amount of plumage on his broad-brimmed hat, I spoke with remarkable calmness.

'Good morning, Sir Roger.'

'Good morning, Mr Devarre,' he replied, coldly polite. 'May I introduce Doctor Russell?'

The doctor was a gaunt figure with a short grey beard, about fifty years of age.

'Good morning,' he said crisply and, much to my surprise, shook my hand as I returned his greeting.

'Let's go to the field on the other side of the trees,' said Sir Roger.

We proceeded through three rows of trees and a few thorn bushes, disturbing a stag and two does which headed off at a gallop. Once beyond the trees, we halted on the verge of a vast green meadow, and Sir Roger removed his cloak. The day was dawning fast.

Doctor Russell opened a shallow wooden case he had brought from the carriage. Two identical long-barrelled, flintlock pistols were securely housed within the red velvet interior.

'Now, Mr Devarre,' he addressed me in businesslike tones. 'I have carefully loaded both of these pistols with an equal charge and a single ball. As the challenged party, you have the right to first choice of weapon, and you can thereby be certain that there cannot have been any malpractice on our part.'

'Thank you,' I said.

Even though I trusted the doctor, I picked the pistol furthest from me. Sir Roger took the remaining one and perused it for a moment.

'Let's get it done,' he said brusquely.

'Very well,' said the doctor. 'Stand back to back.'

We took up that position with our pistols in our right hands pointed upwards. I can remember thinking that although I strongly believed in honour, there were occasions when men maintained that concept to the point of lunacy.

The doctor enquired, 'Is twenty paces agreeable to you both?'

We answered that it was.

'You will both march ten paces, then halt and face one another. Off you go.'

I marched ten paces, as instructed, and turned round to face my adversary, now twenty paces away. Advisedly, I stood with my right side towards him in order to present a slimmer target, Sir Roger adopting the same posture.

'Fully cock your weapons,' the doctor called.

I pulled the hammer of my pistol all the way back to full cock and checked the frizzen's upright position.

Doctor Russell issued his final instruction. 'When I drop my handkerchief, you will both fire.'

It was now almost fully light, and I could see Sir Roger quite clearly. I felt extremely reluctant to fire at another human being for no good reason. But then an image formed in my mind of him mounting my darling Corinne the previous night and, believe me, readers, I was ready to shoot.

Doctor Russell held a large white handkerchief out in front of him at eye-level. Waiting was hard to bear. Suddenly, the white silk fell from his hand.

I took quick aim at my opponent's right shoulder and pressed the trigger. The hammer flint sparked and there was a flash and wisp of smoke from the priming pan – but then nothing. A misfire! Oh, my God!

I heard the detonation of Sir Roger's pistol, saw the smoke and felt a blow in my right eye. The earth and sky began to revolve – then all went dark.

I regained consciousness in the carriage as it speeded away from the scene of our indulgence in an activity that had been illegal since 1666; but I was aware only of the pain in my eye socket and Doctor Russell bending over me, staunching the flow of blood with gauze pads. I have no recollection of Sir Roger's presence – although I presume he must have travelled with us as far as his mansion in Pall Mall – nor of anything else about that journey. I may well have lost consciousness again.

Doctor Russell took me to an establishment in Covent Garden for treatment and recuperation. It was the home of a Mrs Henrietta Langley, who had once been a nurse in St Bartholomew's Hospital, the House of the Poor, but who now provided medical care for the better off at a substantial fee. With the assistance of two other former nurses, she was at that time caring for seven patients, each with his own private room. The doctor told me that the lead ball was lodged within my destroyed right eye but could easily be removed. He then gave me a draught of brandy, carefully extracted the ball with forceps and cleaned up the wound, unavoidably causing me great pain. Mrs Langley then dressed the wound and gave me two opium pills which rendered me oblivious to the pain and to everything around me. I was later surprised to learn that all of my medical fees had been discharged by Sir Roger Trevanyon.

I remained in Mrs Langley's care for a week until the wound was sufficiently healed, experiencing from time to time considerable pain and discomfort, both from my wound and from the ointments she applied to it. When I returned home to Highgate, I consulted Doctor Elisha Coysh, who lived in a picturesque cottage halfway down Swine's Lane. He verified that my wound was healing satisfactorily and confirmed Doctor Russell's opinion that I would require no further treatment, unless there were any later indications of further damage. It was now just a question of getting used to viewing the world with one eye and accepting the discomfort the other useless one might continue to give me for a while. At least, I was still alive.

19

In the days that followed, I remained depressed about the loss of my eye, and even more so that my beloved Corinne had now been snatched permanently out of my life, just as Harriet Abercorn and Mary Blakeney had been. I spent many hours of every day thinking about Corinne, remembering our happy times together and dreaming about what might have been. And on occasions when I called in at the Gatehouse Tavern, I was poor company for my two drinking companions, Jeremy Grenville and Timothy Cottle. Although Jeremy was understanding of what ailed me, Timothy was inclined to complain bluntly that I should cheer up. This, however, was not easy to do. Even a letter from William Crooke, Temple Bar, informing me that *A Pirate for Harriet* would be published the following month, was unable to dispel my misery.

Finally, on Thursday morning, 7 October 1669, in a desperate bid to find a means of raising my spirits, I dressed in my favourite dove-grey velvet coat and dark grey plumed hat and travelled by public coach to London.

It was a bright, sunny day and warm for the time of year. I first dined in the Rose Tavern on the east corner of Brydges Street, adjacent to Old Drury Theatre. In a private room, where I would not be disturbed by boisterous young gallants feasting and drinking in the taproom, I ate a splendid dinner. Stewed carp, jowl of salmon and pullet in almond sauce, complemented by a flask of Provence wine, fortified me well for the afternoon ahead. It was my intention to take pleasure with some buxom young strumpet, of which there were multitudes in this district.

Readers may wonder why I am not habitually expressing concern about the dangers to my immortal soul, as I so often did in my previous memoir. The answer is that I had now sinned so many times, one way and another, that I could see no point in further concerning myself about the matter. Either my soul was already irretrievably condemned or the Good Lord Jesus, having died for our sins upon the cross, might intercede for me, considering I have always been a person of benevolent and kindly intentions.

But it was certainly with sinful intent that I left the Rose Tavern and turned right into Russell Street, heading for Drury Lane. The cobbled road was thick and rank with mire and garbage. Like others on foot, I kept close to the wall to avoid the passing carriages, as well as the carts and barrows, loaded with fruit and vegetables, on their way to Covent Garden. Hardly had I gone a few yards, however, when a young woman stepped from the shadow of one of the timber-framed Tudor buildings and grasped my arm.

'Are you seeking pleasure on this lovely afternoon, sir?' she enquired.

Surprised by her clear and cultivated voice, I stopped and looked at her closely. My one eye swiftly took in the dark mantle and blue velvet gown with white lace frills on the low, scooped neckline of the bodice. Black silken ringlets flowed beneath the broad brim of her hat. Before her face she held a black vizard mask.

'If pleasure has a pleasing look,' I replied.

She lowered her mask.

Shocked? Horrified? Astounded?

No words can possibly describe my reaction to the features thus revealed. Flawless, olive complexion – pale

158

blue eyes – exquisite beauty. Impossible though it seemed, there was no doubt about it.

'Mistress Blakeney!' I exclaimed with a gasp.

Mary Blakeney frowned and looked at me closely.

'Why, Mr Devarre!' she cried, clearly surprised, though not as much as I had been. 'I didn't recognise you with that black eye-patch.'

'In God's name, Mary,' I said. 'What has brought you to this?'

'I'm not going to recite my woes to you in the street, Mr Devarre,' she replied in tones reminiscent of her old, haughty attitude towards me. 'I am a working girl and you are a potential customer. Are you seeking pleasure or not?'

'Very well,' I said sharply. 'Consider yourself hired for the afternoon. Come with me.'

She dutifully followed me back into the Rose Tavern. I led the way past some central oak tables, around which sat gaudily clad, inebriated gallants, all talking at once, yet managing to roar with laughter at each other's jests. The ladies of the town, seated amongst them, were resplendent in silks and satins; they flirted wildly and paid little heed to exploring hands. At other tables adjacent to the walls, men in more modest attire supped their ale and smoked their white clay pipes, observing the antics at the central tables with obvious fascination.

Reaching the bar, I addressed the tavern-keeper.

'I wish to hire the same room for another hour, Mr Long.'

'You've chosen well there, Mr Devarre,' he answered. 'Dusky Mary has real class.'

'Dusky Mary?'

'That's what the wags call her because of her skin colour.'

Mary's olive skin and decidedly black hair were inherited

159

from her Italian mother who had died when she was a child.

'Send in a bottle of Malago sack, will you, Mr Long?' I requested.

'Of course, Mr Devarre.'

I paid him a crown and a shilling and took Mary into the private room, where we sat facing one another across the oak table. A potboy promptly knocked on the door and brought in the sack and two glasses. As he departed, I filled the glasses and handed one to Mary. I noted that she drank with the ease of someone who had become accustomed to imbibing. She would now be twenty years old, I considered as I glanced with considerable pleasure at the firm swell of her bosom above the lace neckline of her bodice.

'What happened to your eye, Mr Devarre?' Mary enquired as she lowered the glass from her lovely red lips.

'I lost it two weeks ago in a duel,' I replied.

'That is truly unfortunate,' she said with some sympathy.

'It is even more unfortunate that a refined young lady like yourself has been reduced to selling her body on the street,' I said. 'How did this come to be, Mary?'

She hesitated for a moment, then shrugged her shoulders.

'It can do no harm to tell you, I suppose. As you will already know, my father had to sell our mansion in Highgate, and we moved to a small rented house in Duck Lane. But this availed him little. His financial situation was far worse than he had told me. After his food importing business had been dissolved, his creditors kept hounding him and, six months ago, he was committed to the Clink, that ancient prison in Southwark, as a debtor. Oh, Mr Devarre, it is terrible in there! The prisoners are all shackled and live crammed together in filth and excrement, with rats and cockroaches everywhere. There is constant uproar and regular violence, and there are many deaths from disease. My father's debts amount to nearly nine thousand pounds which he can not possibly pay. He has no hope of release from that filthy, disgusting place.

'I had to pay the gaoler sixpence to be permitted to visit. And one day, my father told me if I could pay the gaoler sixteen shillings a week, he could get a cell on his own with a bed. He was sure he would die if he remained incarcerated amongst that foul and violent rabble, many of whom were transferred there from Newgate prison at the time of the Great Fire.'

Mary paused to drink the rest of her sack. I refilled both our glasses and she drank some more.

'So what could I do, Mr Devarre? The money I had obtained from selling my jewellery was now gone. I was penniless and desperately in need of funds to keep him alive, pay my rent and feed myself. My father gave me a letter to take to Madam Ross in Lewkenor's Lane...'

'It was your father's idea?' I interrupted her, astonished.

'Yes, it was. I have not always seen eye to eye with my father, although I have at all times been obedient to him, but in this instance, after my initial horror, I came to see there was really no alternative. I knew I had to obtain an immediate income, and I would never have been able to earn sufficient money working as a chambermaid or doing some other menial task. I really had no choice. You must see that, Mr Devarre.'

'I understand,' I said uncertainly.

Perhaps Mary felt she had no choice, but surely her father could have chosen to continue to live in squalor and danger, and if necessary to die, rather than send his own daughter to become a common whore? I had never liked Alexander Blakeney, any more than he had liked me, but I still loved his daughter. Oh yes. I loved Mary every bit as much as I had when I used to take my morning strolls through the village, hoping for even a glimpse of her. My passion for Corinne had certainly overshadowed that devotion during the past year, but it had never extinguished it.

Mary seemed to take some pride in her next statement.

'Madam Ross was very pleased to get me and priced me higher than any of her other girls. So if you are hiring me for the afternoon, Mr Devarre, I will have to charge you five guineas.'

I took another drink as I considered the situation.

'I don't wish to pay that price,' I said firmly.

'You can't expect to have someone of my quality for any less,' she retorted haughtily.

'I'm going to offer you more, not less.'

Mary smiled for the first time since our meeting and I was instantly enraptured by the radiance this brought to her comely face.

'More?' she said. 'That's fine. How much d'you consider I'm worth?'

'Nine thousand pounds,' I replied calmly.

The smile disappeared from her face.

'Mr Devarre, I have no time for silly jests. If you are not intent on serious business, I must take my leave and find someone who is.'

'I can assure you, Mary, I *am* being serious. I'm not offering to pay you nine thousand pounds for ten minutes behind a tree in Lincoln's Inn Fields. But I will certainly make such a payment to discharge your father's debts and secure his release from prison – and yours from a life of degradation.'

Mary regarded me in wide-eyed astonishment.

'You really *are* serious, aren't you?' she said at last.

'Absolutely.'

'But why?'

'Mary, I know you are unable to return the love I have for you. Indeed, you always made it clear you didn't find me in the least appealing. But true love is about giving, not receiving. So I wish to give you my love in the only way available to me. I trust you will accept my offer? Believe me, Mary, I will rejoice if you do.'

She continued to look amazed and bewildered.

'What kind of a man are you, Mr Devarre?'

'You just don't understand, do you, Mary?'

'No. I must confess I don't. In bygone days, I considered you a strange individual and found your admiration of me extremely annoying. I did eventually learn that you were a well mannered and kindly intentioned person, but now I find you are quite mad.'

'All people in love are mad,' I said with a slight smile. 'Perhaps you will learn that for yourself one day. But will you accept my offer?'

'Of course I'll accept it,' she replied without hesitation. 'In my present circumstances, I'd be a fool not to.'

'Excellent!' I exclaimed. 'I'll take you to see Mr Crawley, my goldsmith adviser, this very afternoon to arrange for your father's debts to be paid. I'll also give you a little extra to provide for you both until your father finds suitable employment. The East India Company are always seeking people with trading experience. I don't doubt he could secure a position working for them.'

'I am, of course, most grateful for your extraordinary generosity, Mr Devarre,' Mary said, still clearly finding my gesture difficult to comprehend. 'If you would care to come with me now to the house of Madam Ross, or wherever else you may prefer, I will give you your pleasure for as long as you may desire.'

I looked into her eyes which still conveyed little warmth, though her lovely olive complexion, sensuous lips and gently curved bosom strongly aroused my passion for her. Yet I was restrained by the realisation that it was not Dusky Mary, the harlot, that I wanted, but the pure and virtuous maiden whose beauty and stately carriage had captivated my heart nearly three years before and about whom I had dreamed ever since. If I took her now in return for a financial payment, I would lose everything.

'No, Mary,' I said. 'I greatly desire you, but I do not wish to buy your favours. The nine thousand pounds is a testament of my unconditional love. I will not allow this to be sullied.'

Mary eyed me carefully and took another drink of sack.

'Then let me say this to you, Mr Devarre,' she declared. 'In the last six months, I have lain with sundry gentlemen, some of whom have subjected my body to the grossest of indecencies. All of this I have permitted, subject to extra payments of much needed money. But at no time did I allow any of them to kiss me. Indeed, in all my life I have never been kissed by any man. My lips have retained their virtue. Therefore, in return for your unfathomable kindness, permit me to grant you something that cannot be bought.'

Without further ado, she leaned forward across the table towards me and pursed her crayoned lips. With my heart beating faster, I leaned forward also, finding it hard to believe this was really happening. Mary's eyes closed as my lips pressed upon hers. Gradually yielding, her sensual mouth stimulated my senses to the verge of dizziness.

When she drew back, I noted there was no sign of warmth or pleasure in her eyes, but I was not dismayed. I had kissed Mary and for one supreme moment had possessed the remaining vestige of the virtuous young goddess of my dreams. Believe me, dear readers, it was worth every penny of my nine thousand pounds.

'Thank you, Mary,' I said. 'I'll remember that kiss always.'

'Are you really content with nothing more, Mr Devarre?' she asked.

164

'Oh yes, Mistress Blakeney,' I replied. 'I am very content.'

I sat back now and raised my glass to drink. Content I truly was. Through hardships and tragedies, I had gained a fortune in gold for a lady I loved – all in vain. But now, my hard-won fortune was going to rescue this lovely, if distant, young woman whom I had at last kissed and who would always have a place in my heart. My guardian angel had surely guided me well, and for once in my life I had not failed.

20

I returned to Highgate village that evening, very pleased with my most extraordinary and momentous day. 'That Devil-cursed gold,' as Nancy had described it, had been largely donated to what I regarded as a most worthy cause. Mr Crawley had assured me that a letter from him to the Clink prison, guaranteeing the payment of Mr Blakeney's debts, would be sufficient to ensure that unworthy gentleman's immediate release. Mary's delight was as great as Mr Crawley's bemusement at my romantic gesture.

I assumed I would see no more of Mary, but I knew she would continue to be adored in my memory, as would my darling Corinne and the incomparable Harriet Abercorn. I can assure my valued readers that I will undoubtedly love all three of these ladies 'until death and beyond', as I had once declared to Harriet.

After alighting from the stage coach at the top of Holloway Hill, I proceeded to the Angel Inn and seated myself at my favourite table in the alcove adjacent to the entrance door. A log fire blazed cheerily in the fireplace opposite, and as yet there were few customers sitting at other tables. The serving wench, Lucinda – as always with untidy spirals of dark hair and bulging bodice – brought me over a tankard of Alderman Byde's ale. As she placed it upon the table, she gave a little gasp.

'Oh, Mr Devarre,' she exclaimed. 'You look like a pirate with that black patch over your eye.'

'Thank you, Lucinda,' I smiled. 'You'd be surprised how pleased I am to hear that.'

Lucinda frowned; not knowing about my frequent irritation upon finding people skeptical that someone of my appearance and manner could ever have been a pirate.

'How have things been with you, Lucinda?' I enquired, and took a sup of my ale. 'Are you still pining for Jeremy?'

'Not any longer, I'm not,' she replied. 'Why should I keep crying for what's gone? I'm getting wed soon to Tom Perkins, the groom from Sherrick's farmhouse. Maybe 'e don't make me sigh like what Jeremy did, but out of all them what I've kept company with, 'e's the one I can be sure would never let me down.'

Lucinda's words came to me like a revelation from heaven, but this time, I was certain, a true one. I grabbed her hand and kissed it.

'Oh, Mr Devarre,' she uttered coyly.

'Thank you, Lucinda,' I exclaimed. 'You're my true guardian angel.'

So it came to be that four days later, having put my affairs hastily in order, I eagerly boarded a ship at Butolph's Wharf that would take me back to Port Royal and the one woman I could be sure would never let me down.

Certainly the voyage was once more long and tiresome and rendered me seasick on occasions, but my spirits remained high, even jubilant, as I contemplated what lay ahead of me. At long last I would be able to hold Nancy's magnificently voluptuous body in my arms and make entry into her wondrous aperture, as I customarily regarded that part of the female anatomy. I had no doubt this would give me untold joyous satisfaction, even though aware that Jonathon Kincaid, Rory McMullen and two thousand others had preceded me within that much frequented orifice.

I hoped this delight would take place on the night of my arrival, considering how desperately Nancy had pleaded that I should bed her before my departure. After that, as soon

167

as it could be arranged, we would get married in D'Oyley's oak church as Nancy had suggested, no doubt before a congregation of buccaneers and whores, with perhaps a few merchants and government officials also attending. And there would surely be a riotous celebration afterwards at the Sea Horse Tavern, continuing throughout the night.

Leaning against the poop bulwark, looking out over the seemingly endless Atlantic Ocean, or lying in my uncomfortable wooden bed at night, I pictured it all with ever increasing joy and anticipation. Once Nancy and I were wed, we could buy a plot of land for thirty-five pounds or so, upon which we could have a house built according to our requirements, or perhaps purchase and refurbish some existing dwelling. Even after my substantial donation to Mary, I retained a sufficient amount of my gold and inheritance to be considered a fairly wealthy man, and Nancy had a most profitable return from her tavern. Our future would surely be secure.

Although I had grown very fond of Nancy and greatly desired her, I was not in love with her, nor ever could be. But perhaps for this very reason I would be able to live more happily with her, and there was little doubt in my mind that Nancy would be a dutiful and faithful wife as she had so earnestly promised me. Despite her immoral and often sordid past, she had appeared to me to have a deep yearning to become respectable and to be regarded as such, and thereby put behind her all that had previously befallen her. From now on, it would be my mission to help her do exactly that.

At long last, on the afternoon of Monday, 13 December 1669, I stepped ashore in Port Royal harbour with a glad heart, and shortly afterwards eagerly presented myself in the smoky, rumbustious Sea Horse Tavern. William Carbury, Nancy's burly but well spoken assistant manager, looked up from behind the bar as I approached.

'Why, Nathaniel – back so soon?' he exclaimed in surprise. 'God's blood! What happened to your eye?'

'I lost it in a duel,' I said cheerily. 'Good to see you again, William. Is Nancy upstairs?'

'No, I'm afraid not, Nathaniel,' he answered grimly. 'Nancy is dead.'

I heard the words, but for a moment was unable to accept them.

'Dead?'

'I am sorry to say she is, Nathaniel. The morning after you left, she had a sudden attack of the shakes and took to her bed, alternately shaking and sweating. The doctor wasn't sure what ailed her. There was no yellowing of the skin or eyes, so it wasn't yellow fever. He said it must have been something that had got into her bloodstream in the Tabasco swamps, but he thought it odd the fever had taken twelve days to develop. By nightfall, she had become delirious and within four days, she was dead.'

It *was* true then. Nancy was dead!

William grasped one of the tankards he had been filling with kill-devil and placed it before me. I drank deeply.

'Could it have been malaria?' I asked.

William shook his head.

'The doctor didn't think so. He said this fever didn't fit the normal pattern. And I'll tell you something else. Just before she died, Nancy suddenly ceased her incoherent babbling and for a few moments became lucid. She looked up at me and said, "Oh, it's you, William." Her face was pale and drawn and soaked in perspiration, and her eyes seemed tormented as she said, "I always kenned Hootsyposhty would get me." Her strength then left her and she died a minute later with her eyes staring wildly, as though she'd seen the Devil himself.'

'It's all a terrible tragedy,' I sighed. 'Nancy was obsessed with a superstitious fear of Huitzlipochtli's revenge. That very obsession could have helped to kill her, but the principal cause must have been some swamp fever.'

What I did *not* say to William was that Nancy had been yet another victim of my obsessive passion for Corinne. This tragic death would weigh even more heavily upon my conscience than the others. I was certainly being punished for my sins. First, my dreams of happiness with Corinne had been shattered, then I'd lost my right eye, now my planned joyous union with Nancy had been cruelly snatched away. Yet, in all honesty, I couldn't complain that I didn't deserve these misfortunes, and I still don't complain. I plead guilty, dear Lord. I have sinned grievously. But I have always meant well.

I arranged with William to take up residence in my old room. That night, I had a few drinks with my faithful shipmate, Zebediah Watkins, which cheered me up considerably, and later shared my bed with the African harlot known as Jumping Joyce – so named because of her dancing agility. And, in this way, I was presented with a disquieting new factor to ponder.

Joyce and I lay together in the darkness, covered by a sheet to provide our naked bodies with some protection against the inevitable mosquitoes. Nancy was still very much on my mind, and I shared my thoughts with my bedmate.

'I had expected to sleep tonight with Nancy. It's still hard to believe she died of that fever so quickly.'

To my surprise, Joyce answered, 'Missee Nancy not kill by de fever, Cap'n Devra. Her kill by de brown man priest. Him put de spell on her. Him kill her.'

'How can you say that?' I asked scornfully.

'I see it many times in Nigeria. De witch doctor make de spell and someone die.'

'But the brown man priest is hundreds of miles from here.'

170

'Him make de spell at any distance. I see it happen plenty. And when I take de turn nursing Missee Nancy, I see her empty eyes. Her under de spell. Her have no will of her own. A Yoruba witch doctor kill me mother, Cap'n Devra. Missee Nancy have de same look. De brown man priest kill her. I know.'

I was beginning to feel very disturbed. I didn't believe it, of course – or so I tried to tell myself.

'We talk no more of de bad things,' Joyce now said, wriggling her lithe, ebony body against me. 'You wan' fok me, da'lin, or you just wan' kiss me tits like before?'

She was referring to that drunken occasion two nights prior to my departure for Tabasco, when I danced with her on the table and later brought her up to my room.

'Is that all I did last time?' I enquired with eager interest.

'You not remember? You have too much of de rum. You fall asleep.'

Am I correct in supposing that my readers would like to know what happened this time? Well, mind your own business! All I am prepared to tell you is that it was nothing like the previous occasion.

The following morning – to her surprise and delight – I paid Joyce five gold guineas and sent her on her way, dancing with joy.

After I had partaken of a small breakfast, William Carbury arranged for Nancy's carriage to take me along the lengthy, bustling High Street to the eastern limit of the town, and onwards through the Palisadoes gate to the cemetery which lay beyond. Here were buried Port Royal's dead – mostly victims of smallpox, yellow fever, tuberculosis, dysentery, and other alcohol-related ailments.

Following the directions William had given me, I had no trouble in locating Nancy's grave. William told me that Nancy's funeral was well attended by some of Port Royal's more respectable residents, as well as by a large

171

gathering of sea rovers and strumpets. I looked now at the simple headstone and read the words carved there:

NANCY MONCRIEFF

DIED 28TH JULY 1669

AGED 28

HER SHORT LIFE WAS

DEDICATED TO

PROVIDING MEN WITH

PLEASURE

MAY SHE RECEIVE HER

REWARD IN HEAVEN

I liked this inscription and decided to commend William on his choice of words. And, at long last, I had learned Nancy's surname. For some reason, she never divulged it and nobody else seemed to know what it was. I could only suppose William must have come across it in her personal papers.

I removed my hat, bowed my head and prayed aloud.

'Almighty God, I give thee hearty thanks for this thy servant, whom thou hast delivered from the miseries of this wretched world, and, as I trust, hast brought her soul, committed into thy holy hands, into sure consolation and rest. Amen.'

After making the sign of the cross, I replaced my hat and stood in silence for a few moments. Then I spoke again, hopeful that by some means my words would reach Nancy, wherever she might be.

'Well, dear Nancy, I returned to Port Royal hoping to make you my wife, only to find that a cruel fate had taken you from me. I promise you, my esteemed and desired Nancy, I shall never forget you.'

Thus I said goodbye to a truly courageous and remarkable woman. Certainly she could be hard and undoubtedly crude, but she had a good and generous heart which, I dared to believe, she had finally given to me. This was the one part of her anatomy she had never offered to any man before – rather as Mary had presented me with her virgin lips. So I supposed I could say I'd had *some* success with women!

I laughed quietly, as I was inclined to do at my own jests, and felt strangely at peace. Looking northwards across the calm blue sea of the inlet towards the green coastal plain and the Blue Mountains beyond, I marvelled at Jamaica's majestic beauty and resolved, there and then, to remain awhile. Much as I loved it, there was no urgency to return to my home in Highgate. All morning I had been aware of a compulsion to write a second memoir of my adventures and misfortunes, and this task could be undertaken perfectly well here in Port Royal. At the same time, perhaps I could commence work on a project I had envisaged during the voyage over. This was to produce an assemblage of paintings of everyday life in Port Royal, comprising portraits of buccaneers, whores and other local characters, together with a few street and harbour scenes. Most certainly included would be interior and exterior representations of the Sea Horse Tavern, with Nancy painted from memory.

These two activities would keep my mind occupied and would, no doubt, have a restorative effect, healing my wounded heart and soothing my troubled soul. I would eventually return to England, but in the meantime – provided Huitzlipochtli didn't get me – I would have writing and painting to content me during the daytime, and kill-devil and Jumping Joyce at night. Who could ask for more?

The sun was now at its zenith, but a cooling breeze

blew in from the sea. I took a deep breath. Despite all the sorrow and pain of this unpredictable and treacherous world, it was good to be alive.

21

During my sojourn in Port Royal I found myself unexpectedly involved in great and historic events. It would require a whole book to present my readers with a detailed description of my experiences during these months, but a concise account of this interlude in my tale of amorous folly must suffice.

In June 1670, following an increase in harassment of English shipping, Spanish corsairs raided the north-west coast of Jamaica, burning settlements and killing and capturing a number of English inhabitants. The enraged governor of the island, Sir Thomas Modyford, sanctioned a renewal of defensive hostilities against the Spanish, and commissioned Admiral Henry Morgan to take command of such operations. The secret that the Admiral was planning a crippling blow against Spanish dominion in the New World soon became common knowledge in Port Royal as Morgan's captains scoured the taverns seeking a willing force of men.

When Colonel Lawrence Prince told me one day that he was in need of a navigator aboard his ship, the *Pearle*, I did not hesitate to sign up with him. In my heart I still considered myself a buccaneer, and I now felt bound to accompany the Brethren of the Coast upon what promised to be the greatest attack they had ever mounted against the Spanish Empire. Unfortunately, Zebediah would not be coming with me. He had used his gold to purchase a grog shop which he now ran with a plump and pleasant widow whom he was soon to wed.

At that time, I had written twenty chapters of this memoir and completed twenty-seven paintings of persons and places in Port Royal which, though not great works of art, were nonetheless most pleasing to me. There was now nothing to keep me in Jamaica, though Jumping Joyce was not happy about my departure. She said she would miss me, but I suspect it was my generous payments she would miss the most.

The *Pearle* was a square-rigged vessel of 50 tons, twelve guns and a crew of 70, with whom I got along surprisingly well. We joined other ships from Jamaica and Tortuga beginning to gather at the Ile-à-Vache, off the south-western tip of Hispaniola. Protected by a dangerous reef with a narrow channel permitting entrance to the principal bay, this little island was an ideal rendezvous, having also a freshwater lake close to the bay and a secluded cavern on the coast in which Morgan could store supplies and munitions.

It was within one of the limestone tunnels of this cavern that Colonel Prince introduced me to the great man himself. Morgan was robust and broad-shouldered, with a curling moustache and a small point of beard upon his chin. His bold eyes twinkled merrily as he greeted me in his Welsh accent.

'Ah, Nathaniel Devarre. I've heard all about you. You once sailed with Jonathon Kincaid and you were a friend of poor Nancy, were you not? Well, she was a handsome figure of a woman, generous of bust and heart. Many's the jolly gallop I had on her in years gone by. But, look you, don't mention a word of this to my wife.'

He guffawed with laughter and I felt compelled to laugh with him, desite annoyance at his no doubt truthful assertion about Nancy. I was, nonetheless, to become considerably impressed by him. Loud and forthright in speech and manner, he had a powerful presence and a charismatic command of men which I admired throughout the expedition.

After some initial mishaps and delays, we eventually set sail on Thursday, 18 December 1670. It was the largest buccaneer fleet ever assembled, comprising 38 ships and 2,000 men, about a third of whom were French. Morgan had resolved to carry out an audacious strategic strike against the prestigious and wealthy city of Panama on the southern coast of the Isthmus of Darien. Commanded by Colonel Bradley, an advance party of three ships and 470 men first captured the fortress of San Lorenzo at the mouth of the Chagres River on the northern coast, with the loss of 30 buccaneers and 360 Spanish soldiers.

Leaving 300 men to garrison this castle and guard our ships, we then set out on Monday, 19 January 1671 – 1,500 strong – up the winding river in five shallow-draught sloops and 36 boats and canoes, carefully avoiding mangrove roots, fallen tree trunks and sandbanks. On the fourth day, we had to leave our boats, with 200 men to guard them, and proceed on foot, cutting our way through the dense forest of palm, mahogany and giant cedar trees, thorn bushes and woven webs of creepers.

We marched for seven days through this humid wilderness, enduring torrential rainstorms and periodically having to ward off alligators, snakes, and poisonous insects, and regularly tormented by the all too familiar leeches and mosquitoes. I have to say that when you are having to contend with such dangers and discomforts, while close to exhaustion, you take little pleasure in the occasional beauties of scarlet blossoms, richly plumed parrots or brightly-coloured humming-birds.

Colonel Prince had appointed me Captain of musketeers, which I was pleased to find was well received by the men under my command. On the march, we carried our muskets smeared with lard and wrapped in greasy cloths to preserve

177

them from rain and swamps. Our powder was secured in corked flasks or bottles, and those men with matchlock muskets stored their slow matches in glass jars.

From the start, we were subjected to sporadic harassment from hostile Indians who fired their poisoned arrows from the cover of the surrounding foliage and, on occasions, sprang ambushes which cost us not a few lives. But our greatest losses were from sickness. Hundreds of men became victims of malaria and yellow fever; many died.

There was also hunger. Thinking we would find food along the way, we had carried few provisions, but were soon made aware of our grave miscalculation. The Spanish garrisons encountered on our route along the mule caravan trail from Portobello to Panama always abandoned their positions and fled, confining their resistance to brief skirmishing and sniping. During this retreat, they carried off all foodstuffs and destroyed crops and anything else of use from the villages, burning the houses so that we would be provided with no shelter. Consequently, we suffered terribly from hunger and many men ate their own boots, soaking, scraping, boiling and slicing up the leather. I managed to survive by eating snails, beetles and grasshoppers, but the gnawing pains in my stomach were severe. A goodly number wanted to turn back but, by the sheer force of his personality and crude but powerful oratory, Henry Morgan persuaded them to continue.

By Tuesday, 27 January 1671, sickness and hostile action had reduced our numbers by as many as 300 men, but on that day we at last arrived upon the vast plain which lay before Panama City and the coast of the South Sea. Here, to our delirious delight, we came upon a large herd of cattle and consequently gorged ourselves on beef – in most cases before it was adequately roasted – so great was our hunger.

The following morning, we were confronted on this

grassland by all the forces the Governor of Panama could muster. Mostly militia and predominantly mixed race or black, 1,200 foot soldiers were drawn up in a long formation, six deep, with 200 horsemen on each flank. Henry Morgan's leadership and initiative proved exemplary. At the outset, he sent 300 men along a gully to occupy a small hill on the Spanish right. Colonel Prince was in joint command of the vanguard of our three remaining squadrons, each 300 strong and bearing red and green buccaneer flags in addition to the English colours.

It was Morgan's plan to wait for the enemy to attack, advancing into the sun. A body of Spanish cavalry shortly obliged and charged down upon us. Our concentrated volleys of musket fire, ranks firing and reloading alternately, sent men and horses tumbling into the grass. Our men on the flanking hill – many of them French marksmen – directed deadly fusillades into the mass of neighing, distraught horses and their undoubtedly brave riders. The Spanish infantry now broke ranks, charging through us to attack Morgan's main body. Most of them were poorly armed but nonetheless engaged us in desperate and bloody combat. We chopped many down with our cutlasses, and it was not long before the survivors were retreating in complete disorder.

In final desperation, the Spanish ordered Indians and Negroes to stampede two herds of cattle into our rear squadron, but well-aimed musket fire easily turned them around and drove many of the terror-stricken beasts back amongst the fleeing enemy. Our trumpeters and drummers then signalled the advance. During our pursuit, blood lust possessed the buccaneers, so that between four and five hundred Spanish soon lay dead or badly wounded. Miraculously, our own losses in this battle were but five dead and ten wounded.

However, our victory was to reap comparatively little material reward. Retreating soldiers and slaves, carrying out the Governor's orders, ignited gunpowder deposits, setting fire to the city, much of which was thereby destroyed. Three large ships, loaded with most of Panama's gold, silver, jewels and other treasures, had already put to sea, bound for Ecuador.

For four weeks we searched what remained of the city and its outlying areas, seeking any concealed riches and – I have since learned – failing to identify a solid gold altar which resourceful friars had painted white. Torture of prisoners to extract information was excessive, both by buccaneer and Spanish standards, and certainly there were acts of rape perpetrated upon the unfortunate women who had fallen into our hands. I should perhaps point out, however, that, generally speaking, buccaneers are no more wicked than soldiers of all nations, who regularly indulge in such despicable behaviour when given the opportunity. I might also add that a number of Spanish women appeared to succumb with little resistance.

Towards the end of our time in Panama, something occurred which gave me considerable satisfaction. One night, whilst drinking wine with Colonel Prince and a couple of his close associates in the Governor's undamaged stone house near the harbour, Henry Morgan took me aside and said confidentially:

'Nathaniel, I know you to be a person of intelligence and sensitivity. I wish to ask your advice on a matter that is deeply troubling me. I have a rampant desire for a young and beautiful Spanish lady, but she is very chaste, look you, and all of my efforts to woo her have come to naught. Her husband is attending to business in Peru and her intended ransome money has gone astray. I simply don't know what I should do about her.'

'Why don't you release her?' I suggested.

'Release her?' he queried with a frown. 'What would I gain from that?'

'What have you to gain from continuing to hold her prisoner? If she is so chaste and true to her husband, she will never willingly yield to you, no matter what you do. And as you have clearly desisted from taking her by force, I suspect that, in addition to your great desire, you also have a high regard, and possibly even love, for the lady. So why not set her free and send her away thinking well of you instead of ill? Would you not thereby have given expression to your feelings for her in the best way that is available to you, and would it not please you to bc able to remember it so in the years to come?'

He smiled and nodded.

'Indeed it would,' he said. 'By my blood, it would! Nathaniel, you are my trusty friend.'

The following morning, he provided the young lady with a mule to ride and a Negress to attend her, and sent her on her way along the coast to where she would surely find shelter and security amongst her own people until her husband's return from Peru.

We departed from Panama on Tuesday, 24 February 1671 with Spanish prisoners to be ransomed and captured slaves to be sold, and a train of 175 mules laden with gold and silver plate, jewels, silks, lace and linens. But this was far less than the buccaneers had expected to obtain from the legendary transit point of all the gold and silver from the mines of Peru and Potosi. There was much ill feeling verging on mutiny, particularly amongst the French, during the return march across the Isthmus of Darien.

Upon our arrival at Chagres on the northern coast, Admiral Morgan agreed to an immediate division of the booty, estimated at about 30,000 pounds in total value. Each individual share amounted therefore to little more than 16 pounds. The men were outraged by this meagre return for all they had endured. Even though Morgan had ordered everyone, including himself, to be thoroughly searched, accusations of dishonesty continued to be made against him. Rightly fearing for his life, the Admiral quietly slipped away aboard the *Mayflower* on Monday, 16 March 1671, accompanied by three other vessels, including the *Pearle*. Some have claimed that Morgan took an undisclosed portion of the plunder with him. There is no evidence that he did any such thing, and I certainly do not believe he was the type of person who would cheat the men under his command. Most of the remaining ships then went raiding along the coast of Central America, though with little success; a few were wrecked by storms.

When our four ships arrived back in Port Royal on Tuesday, 14 April 1671, we found that the government of England considered we had committed an act of illicit piracy. A new treaty had been signed between England and Spain the previous July to restore peace in the region. Sir Thomas Modyford would later claim that, as soon as he received the news of the treaty, he had attempted to send word to Admiral Morgan to halt his intended expedition. All I can say is that if he did, he can't have tried very hard! Call it patriotism or piracy, I certainly have no regrets that I participated in this great buccaneer adventure which has resulted in such a loss of Spanish prestige that Spain's hegemony of power in the New World has been surely broken and will steadily decline from this time onwards.

The populace of Port Royal, unconcerned by this controversy, flocked to the harbour to welcome us back as heroes. As I stepped onto the quay, delighted and relieved to be back in Jamaica safe and sound, Henry Morgan broke away from a crowd of well-wishers and hastened over to me.

'Nathaniel, I am most grateful for your stalwart service and unfailing loyalty to me,' he said with clear sincerity.

'You are a gentleman worthy of the name and a true buccaneer.'

We parted company with a firm handshake and a mutual declaration that we would both maintain friendly contact, but I knew I would not be remaining in Port Royal for much longer. Though overjoyed by the Admiral's praise of me and proud of my exploits as a buccaneer, I was weary of suffering and bloodshed, and craved the tranquillity of my village in England. All my thoughts were now of home.

22

I arrived home on Wednesday, 24 June 1671, and for the next two months was completely idle. I made no attempt to resume working as a portrait painter and spent my days taking country strolls, drinking in taverns and taking my ease. And I was very content to do so. Only after returning from war does a man appreciate how very precious a peaceful existence can be. But fate was once more about to take me by surprise.

Approaching noon on Thursday, 20 August 1671, I was seated at my desk in my upstairs study, belatedly applying myself to completing this memoir. Periodically looking out through the window before me, my one eye had a pleasing view of the beds of roses and marigolds in my garden, the boundary hedges of briar roses and the bountiful grass and adjacent ponds of Highgate village green.

Comfortably relaxed in white linen shirt and full breeches, my generally contented mood grew disturbed as I revised my account of Nancy's death. This brought other unhappy recollections to the forefront of my mind. Harriet, Mary, Corinne and Nancy were all now gone from my life and here I was, with a destroyed right eye, afraid to socialise with young women for fear of falling in love, only to be rejected.

I was feeling sorry for myself again. Enough of that! My remaining eye was serving me well enough, was it not? And how many men in England could claim to have been a buccaneer and valued associate of Henry Morgan? The occasional harlot would always provide a degree of pleasure, would she not? What had I to complain of?

With my morale sufficiently restored, I once more contemplated the pleasant vista of my garden and the village green. A young woman in a sky-blue hat and gown was approaching along the pathway between the two fenced ponds. Her movements were graceful, even stately...

My God! It was Mary!

Without further thought, I leapt to my feet and rushed downstairs and through the garden. As I stepped out of the wooden gateway, I came abruptly face to face with my first love who, to my surprise, was intent upon calling on me and not merely passing by.

'Good morning, Mistress Blakeney,' I said genially.

'Good morning, Mr Devarre,' Mary replied. 'I do hope I am not disturbing you. There is an important matter I wish to discuss.'

'I wasn't doing anything that can't wait,' I said, surprised that there could be any matter so important she would travel the five miles from London to consult someone whom she had never wished to be a part of her life. On the other hand, I had been of considerable service to her before leaving for Jamaica. Was she, perhaps, in need of more money? 'Won't you come in, Miss Blakeney?'

'Thank you, Mr Devarre,' she said pleasantly. 'But it's such a lovely day, I thought perhaps we could sit out here on the green.'

'Of course.'

We walked together up the earthen pathway to a wooden bench in front of a row of elm trees that marked the boundary of the bowling green which lay behind my house. It was indeed a lovely day, the noon-day sun bathing the village green in warmth and light. We sat down side by side, facing towards the two ponds and the blacksmith's forge, beyond which a shepherd and his dog could be seen ushering a herd of bleating sheep down Holloway Hill.

'It's wonderful to be back here,' Mary said wistfully. 'I do miss those heavenly times when my father and I lived in our mansion on the Toll Road. I was blissfully innocent in those days, Mr Devarre. I only wish I could have remained that way.'

'I was fairly innocent myself at that time,' I said. 'Even though I had served in the navy for eight years and sailed the seas as far as the west coast of Africa, I had still retained much of my innocence when I took up residence here in Highgate. If you don't mind me saying so, Mary, my only sensual pleasure was observing you walking through the village.'

'And I resented your obvious admiration of me. Yet I suppose I should really have regarded it as a compliment.'

I looked into her pale blue eyes which pleasingly contrasted with her flawless, olive complexion, and was instantly possessed by a deep longing.

'You were a truly beautiful young lady in those days, Mary,' I declared with a tremor in my voice. 'And you still are today.'

'Life was simple in those days,' she said sadly. 'If only fate had not decreed that my father should get so seriously into debt, thereby forcing me into that terrible life of sin.'

I tried to offer her some reassurance. 'It may not give you very much comfort, Mary, but I have considerable respect for women living that life of sin, as you call it. They provide a valuable service – particularly for men who, for one reason or another, are unable to succeed in normal courtship.'

She retorted haughtily, 'No, Mr Devarre, that gives me no comfort at all.'

I quickly changed the subject.

'How is your father now? Is he working again?'

'Oh, yes,' she replied. 'As you suggested he might do,

he managed to obtain employment with the East India Company soon after his release from prison. We again took up residence in rented property in Duck Lane and life was better for a while. But...'

Mary stopped and looked across the green at three young children chasing one another around the lower pond while their nursemaid sharply called to them to come back.

'But what?' I prompted her.

She took a deep breath and continued.

'But a few months ago, my father remarried.'

'Really?' I exclaimed.

'Yes, it was a surprise to me also after all these years. I have to be quite honest, Mr Devarre. I resented this woman's presence in the house from the start and she certainly resented mine. Very shortly, my father began to emphasise that it was about time I was married and living in a home of my own. Consequently, in the last few months he has invited three young men to meet me, none of whom I have found appealing.'

'As was the case with me,' I could not help pointing out.

'Yes. But at that time, I only knew of your strange ways, Mr Devarre, and had yet to learn of the qualities you were later to reveal.'

I was considerably cheered by this statement.

'These three gentlemen were definitely not to my taste, but each one, in turn, seemed eager to pursue a courtship. However, I speedily rid myself of all of them.'

'By what means?'

'On each occasion that my father left me alone with a suitor, I informed him I had once been a whore in Lewkenor's Lane. At that they lost no time in finding an excuse to leave.'

'I can believe it,' I said. 'Last year I returned to Jamaica with the intention of marrying a former whore but,

187

regrettably, she died of a fever before I arrived. However, I don't suppose there are many men in England like me.'

'No, Mr Devarre, there are not. Indeed, I venture to say that there are no men in England quite like you. And I mean that in a positive sense. Your selfless generosity in providing me with a considerable portion of your fortune in gold opened my eyes. When I later had time to consider your gesture, I came to realise all that this entailed.'

'Thank you,' I said, lost for further words.

'Unfortunately, the last of these prospective husbands informed my father of the true reason for his departure. My father was furious and insisted that if he could find another likely suitor, I must remain silent about my past. But, in all honour, I could never deceive anyone in that manner. Marriage should always be undertaken in total honesty. Wouldn't you agree?'

'Ideally, yes.'

'And so I have come here this morning to ask if you would advise me to resolve my problem by marrying Mr Nathaniel Devarre?'

Oh, my cherished readers, do not expect me adequately to describe my feelings upon hearing this question. Amazement … disbelief … bewilderment … all of these. Yet I managed to compose myself and speak calmly.

'What would you suppose this rather unconventional gentleman could offer you?'

'He could provide me with a home in a village that we both love; he could teach me to paint, as so far I have not progressed beyond making crayoned sketches; and he could bestow upon me the eternal love he has always professed to have for me.'

'I see. And what could you offer him?'

'I would be a dutiful wife in every respect, a companion who will understand when he prefers to be alone, and an affectionate and willing recipient of the expression of his love within the marital bed.'

'In that case, Mary,' I said, very conscious of my ardent desire for her, 'if Mr Nathaniel Devarre proposes marriage to you, I strongly advise you to accept.'

Mary smiled. 'And will he propose?'

'Oh, yes. You may be sure of that. But first of all he will wish to pay court to you in the manner you deserve.'

I seized her hand, experiencing a frisson of excitement merely from this innocent contact with her flesh.

'When I take you to the theatre, Mary, if persons around Drury Lane should recognise you from days gone by, we will bid them a hearty good day and I shall be proud to have you on my arm. And one day, I will hire a boat and take you sailing up the Thames. And in a secluded spot along the bank, we will picnic beneath the trees and I will tell you once more how much I love you.'

'And I could read you some of my favourite poetry,' Mary suggested keenly.

'I would like that very much,' I said, and gently kissed her lips. 'I suspect we might find we have much to share with one another.'

Indeed, our courtship progressed very much along these lines. Over the next month, there were visits to the theatre and an idyllic sailing trip up the Thames. But most of all, Mary loved to come to Highgate and stroll with me along the shady avenues of the extensive village green and in woods and meadows further afield. All the while, she appeared to be growing fonder of me but, as with Corinne, I knew she was not actually in love with me. Two years earlier, when her father had intended to offer me her hand in marriage in exchange for my investment in his ailing business, I had told Mary I could live without her love provided I had her kind regard and genuine consent to express my love to her. These conditions had now been met, and surpassed. I was supremely happy and did not have to contend with the constant jealousy with which I had been afflicted during my relationship with Corinne.

It may seem a strange thing to say, but I believe that Mary's months as a Drury Lane strumpet did her a lot of good. Removed from her former sheltered and cosseted existence, immersion in a world of poverty, vulgarity and vice had all but eradicated her previous tendency towards arrogance. She could still on occasions be a little aloof and haughty, but she had now developed a warmer and more understanding side to her nature. That was real progress. I had loved her dearly with all her faults, and now I absolutely adored her.

During our outings in the countryside, we frequently kissed, but at no time did I attempt further intimacy, despite the ever present desire to do so. I was determined to save this delight for our wedding night, so that the bride and groom would then be joined in the flesh for the very first time in the traditional matrimonial manner.

In mid-September, much to Mary's annoyance, her father insisted she accompany his wife and himself to visit her uncle in Oxford. Ten years earlier, Mr Blakeney had violently quarrelled with this brother and severed all relations with him, but the brother had now suggested a reconciliation. During the week that Mary was away, I missed her terribly and resolved I would wait no longer and propose marriage to her immediately upon her return.

On Monday, 28 September 1671, I spent a restful morning in my dining room, which also served as a parlour on the rare occasions I had visitors. It was a bright and pleasant room with wood-panelled walls painted pale cream and a minimum of furniture: an oak table, two cabinets and four chairs. Seated cosily before the flickering flames of the coal burning in the iron fireplace, I was reading a book of John Dryden's poetry which Mary had given me and hoping she might come to see me that very morning.

At a quarter past eleven, sure enough, there came a sharp knocking at my front door, and with great joy I hastened into the hall to admit her. But when I opened the door, it was not Mary standing on the step but the postboy with his customary satchel slung from his shoulder. As I had to pay a charge of three pence for the letter he handed me, I knew it had come more than 80 miles in distance. One glance at the handwriting told me the letter was from Mary. Disappointed that she was not here in person, but pleased to hopefully have news of her imminent arrival, I returned to the living room and sat down again before the fire. After breaking the seal, I unfolded the single sheet of writing paper upon which I read the following:

Oxford, 24 September 1671

Dearest Nathaniel,

It grieves me to write you a letter such as this after all your kindness and devotion to me, but I have a clear duty to delay no longer in doing so.

At my uncle's house in Oxford, I was reunited with my cousin, Ralph, with whom I used to play when we were children. He has grown into a handsome, charming and astute young man and I fell instantly in love with him, as he did with me. I had read about love in books but I never knew it could be so wonderful. And if you are wondering – yes, I have confided in him regarding my unfortunate past, but he has reassured me that he understands the circumstances that drove me to it and admires me all the more for the sacrifice I was prepared to make in order to save my father. When Ralph and I are married, we will make our home here in Oxford.

191

Please forgive me for what you may regard as a betrayal, but I act in all honour, as I had not yet received your proposal of marriage and was therefore not formally promised to you.

I will always remember you, dearest Nathaniel, as someone who turned out to be the finest man I have ever known. Yet it is Ralph who has won my heart and whom I shall therefore wed. May God bless you always.

Your affectionate friend,

Mary

I was so stunned by these words that I immediately read them through a second time in a crazy hope that my mind had been playing tricks on me. But there had been no misconception. It was plainly stated. Mary was no longer to be mine.

No, dear readers, I did not weep. Looking into the gently rising flames, I felt bitter and perplexed that my sublime dream of wedding Mary should be so suddenly extinguished when it seemed on the verge of fruition. Yet it was evident that Mary was now truly happy, and surely that should be my primary concern if I really loved her. Somehow I would have to persuade myself to accept the situation with good grace.

Certainly I was deeply disturbed throughout the remainder of that day and late into the night, and continued so on succeeding days. But as I write these words a month later, I have already raised myself up out of my depression and am determinedly getting on with my life. Yesterday, I went to London to arrange for my services as a portrait painter to be once more advertised by the newspaper, *Mercurius Publicus,* and the Peacock office in The Strand. Afterwards, I ate an excellent dinner at the Rose Tavern and later enjoyed the company of a bright and good-humoured young harlot called Gertrude. Even so, I have to confess that I awoke this morning thinking about Mary.

But, in truth, I have no wish to forget Mary or Harriet or Corinne – or Nancy either. My memories of them are precious and always will be. Nonetheless, as I look out of my study window and survey the green, the trees and the picturesque buildings of my beloved village, it occurs to me that I may gradually learn to no longer resent the pain that love brought me, but only to rejoice in the love that I gave.